THE TRINITY DECEPTION

STONE CHALMERS
BOOK 2

RAYMUND EICH

Copyright © 2025 Raymund Eich

Previously published as *The Greater Glory of God*, **copyright © 2018, 2023 Raymund Eich**

All rights reserved.

No part of this book may be reproduced in any form or by any electronic or mechanical means, including information storage and retrieval systems, without written permission from the author, except for the use of brief quotations in a book review.

Use of any part of this book for the training of any generative AI system, without written permission from the author, is expressly prohibited.

Cover design, book design, and aircraft carrier logo are copyrights, trademarks, or trade dress of CV-2 Books.

ISBN 978-1-952220-23-4

TABLE OF CONTENTS

Prologue	1
Chapter 1	7
Chapter 2	15
Chapter 3	23
Chapter 4	31
Chapter 5	38
Chapter 6	44
Chapter 7	51
Chapter 8	56
Chapter 9	62
Chapter 10	72
Chapter 11	78
Chapter 12	87
Chapter 13	95
Chapter 14	101
Chapter 15	108
Chapter 16	118
Chapter 17	126
Chapter 18	133
Chapter 19	140
Chapter 20	148
Chapter 21	159
Chapter 22	167
Chapter 23	174
Chapter 24	183
Epilogue	188
About the Author	191
Other Books by the Author	193

PROLOGUE

Under the gigantic, yellow and orange banded half-moon high in the sky, Thomas paced a circuit between the main building and the razor wire perimeter fence. He trod a narrow strip of sod, passing from moonlight to the glow of spotlights mounted high on the UN facility's walls. Despite it being early in their planet's three-week long night, sweat clung to his razor bumps. His guard uniform's polyester collar made his neck itch.

You have a job, his mother had said a week earlier in their plastic-walled living room, in the silence after the air conditioner burbled to a stop. The smell of wheat mush on the boil made the modular shanty a home. His infant half-brother slept in a second-hand cradle on the far wall, under the painting of Jesus and His sacred heart. Pride sounded in his mother's voice. *You a better man than all the layabouts in our town. You a better man than the ISTZ devils what sent us here.*

The memory of his mother's voice made Thomas stand taller. He had a job, and he worked for good people. The UN people came to help everyone. Original colonist or recent resettled, it no mattered. His mother and baby brother had running water and cool air, now, thanks to the people come through the wormhole.

Thomas rounded a corner. The building's wall cast a moonshadow cut only by the low, dull lights of the shantytown a kilometer across fallow fields. His gaze darted among pockets of deeper shadow clinging to the facility's recessed windows and a tall, narrow storage tank covered with corrosive and chemical warning pictograms. He found his flashlight by feel and pulled it off his belt with a scritch of hook-and-loop fabric. Tension pierced his shoulders. The noise would alert any bad fellows from the shantytown casing the facility for a burglary.

He thumbed on the flashlight, played the beam over the base of the foamed concrete wall, the underside of the storage tank, the windowsills. Nothing hid in the stark light and jumping sharp-edged shadows.

Thomas slowly exhaled. He slid the beam up the wall, to the spotlight. A jagged hole about the size of an old coin marred the round, frosted white face of the spotlight bulb.

He shook his head, disgust and disappointment dragging down his eyes. Young men from the shantytown sometimes sneaked out to the UN quarter and threw rocks from outside the fences at windows and spotlights. Young men who couldn't find anything better to do but hurt people come to help them. Young men who might be his age, known to him from the football pitch or the stiff wooden pews in church.

Nothing he could do about that, now. Log the damage for the maintenance department to fix tomorrow. He reached for a pocket on the front of his left thigh, unsnapped the flap, reached in. His eyes widened and he shoved his fingers deeper into the pocket, probing each bottom corner. How could he have lost his phone?

Thomas squeezed shut his eyes. He'd showered and changed into his uniform in the locker room before starting his patrol. His phone might be in his other pants or on the locker room floor. If it pleased God, the rubber edge would have kept the phone's screen from breaking.

He would violate his instructions if he went back for his phone now… but mixing up his patrol time could be good, too. Keep the bad fellows from predicting when he'd be in a certain spot. Thomas turned off the flashlight and retraced his steps. His feet quietly padded the sod.

After ducking under a pipe running from a container into the wall, his gaze swept up a stretch of fence obscured by another storage tank's moonshadow. He paused. Not obscured enough. At the bottom of the fence, two strands of barbed wire coiled back from a gap.

He looked up over the storage tank at a spotlight high on the wall. Next to the spotlight, a black splotch covered a camera.

Sweat trickled down Thomas' face. A sliver of cool air chilled his cheek.

Between the tanks, a window hung half an inch above its sill. Inside, alarm wires twisted up like red and black worms.

"Have you started downloading?" asked a voice inside the facility, speaking English in the flat accent of the original colonists. A man, and from his firm tone, in charge.

"Of course I have." Another male voice, but higher and nervous. "I can't rush them, don't rush me, please."

"The Lord knows you can't rush the downloads, but the Devil might get you to slow them down."

The downloader's voice wheedled. "The guard takes ten minutes to stroll the perimeter—"

"Most times," the leader said.

Downloading. The burglars didn't want finished goods from the warehouse and loading docks. They stole plans from the computers.

No. They *tried* to steal plans. Thomas backed away from the window and went around the storage tank. He jogged, keeping his footfalls gentle on the sod. The service door—a steel panel painted a sickly green at the top of three concrete steps—soon came into view.

He padded up the steps, then aimed his thumb toward the print reader beside the door. Stopped before he touched. The print reader would buzz when it unlocked the door, unless he hit the override. He ran his left forefinger along the print reader's edge. A vibration told him he'd found the override. He pressed his fingertip there and laid his right thumb on the print reader.

The door unsealed with a faint thump. Mouth dry, he quietly

turned the handle and pushed the door. The hinges turned soundlessly.

Inside, an empty hallway of long, narrow tiles formed to look like wood. Red emergency exit signs and the idle lights on equipment in lab spaces to right and left provided dim illumination. On quick, light feet Thomas went down the hallway. The roar of his circulating blood filled his ears.

"The drive nozzle download is complete!" The higher-pitched voice broke into a fluttering laugh muffled by a door. Just two rooms ahead on the right. The small room, full of computers, air-conditioned half to freezing.

"Are we done?" The leader's tone commanded attention.

The nervous laugh abruptly ended with a clatter of fingers on computer keys. "I'm looking for airlocks right now."

How could one lock air? No matter, Thomas would keep those designs from these thieves. He pulled a baton from his belt, then crept to the computer room's door. Pressed his thumb against the reader. Tapped a four-digit code on a number pad.

A faint thump. Thomas kicked the door wide and burst into the room. "Hands up!"

In front of him, at a computer screen, a man whipped around his head of shaggy brown hair. Dark saucer eyes. A fish's mouth—

From a corner of the room came a roar. Something punched Thomas in the chest. Another roar, another punch. Again.

Thomas laid his left hand flat on his chest. Pulses of thick liquid gushed between his fingers. A moist iron smell struck his nose and he collapsed.

The other one shot me

From in front of the computer screen, the nervous voice fluttered. "Oh my god oh my god oh my—"

"Quiet," the leader said with a growl. He stepped out of the shadows. A white man as bald as a warlock with a long narrow nose. Eyes in deep sockets regarded Thomas in the computer screen's blue-white glow.

"My god why did you shoot a guard we have to go—"

"Keep. Downloading."

Every inch of Thomas' chest felt burned by acid. His hand clenched on the baton. His mother and baby brother in their tiny house, crying. Never to see them again. *My God, my God, why have you forsaken me?*

"God help us you shot an innocent man—"

For a moment, pity flickered in the deep-socketed eyes. "'Forgive them, Father. They know not what they do.'"

"We have to call an ambulance!"

"Our mission is bigger than one man's life. Keep downloading."

Anger rode the waves of Thomas' gushing blood, then melted. The pain grew distant, throbbing away from him. A bright light filled his inner sight. The light surrounded his mother and infant brother, embracing them with a vast love, vaster than he could show in an entire lifetime of hugging them with his mere arms.

No cry, mama.

The light expanded to embrace Thomas. Then the former things passed away.

CHAPTER 1

At the end of the deep canyon of carbon-nanotube skyscrapers lining Pine Street, early evening sunlight glowed in the memorial gardens. Traffic slowed Stone Chalmers' faceted black coupe to a crawl in the right-turn lane for William Street. Five hundred feet away, across a field as green as a cemetery without headstones, the smooth onyx saddle shape of the nuclear terrorism memorial reflected dazzling light into his eyes. For a moment, the highrises at three corners of the intersection seemed ghosts ready to vanish in a second instant of blinding light.

On the coupe's rear seat next to Stone, his mother squeezed her hands together, rustling her white gold tennis bracelets. "I hate coming so far downtown."

Stone's lips parted in a lazy smile. "It only took forty minutes coming down the FDR."

"You know what I mean." The coupe turned right. On William Street, shadows enveloped the car, but the memorial's afterimage remained a green glow in Stone's retinas. His mother eased her shoulders and peered ahead to the right. "Here we are."

The coupe pulled up in the hotel's passenger dropoff lane and popped its doors. The hum of Lower Manhattan traffic and the hotels' chiller system hit Stone's ears. He climbed out, reached back for his mother. Humid air cloaked them, an extra layer on top of his gray suit and red-and-gold rep tie, on top of his mother's evening dress and the striped, fringed shawl draped over her shoulders.

Stone's gaze darted over the frames and hardware of the hotel's glass doors and windows. Dark discs an inch across and angular cylinders half an inch long revealed themselves to his trained eye. The hotel's security system had more than miniaturized sensors; the servers identified their faces and swung the doors open for them to enter in stride. Conditioned air spilled out and dispelled the humidity like a bad dream.

Inside, a green line, pulsing with arrowheads, appeared on the marble floor in front of them. The hotel's computers negotiated with his implantable computer to induce the vision in his optic nerves through a networked mesh of magnetic stimulators weaved around his hair follicles on his scalp. He walked slowly, his mother's fingers brushing his arm as she matched his pace on chunky heels. The green line ran from the lobby across a twelve-story atrium, around planter boxes and seating alcoves. The line matched the shades of olive leaves and geneteched leather upholstery. They entered a wide corridor carpeted in deep maroon and ended at a pair of propped-open doors, next to a full-color e-ink sign announcing *North American Society for Traditional Reform Judaism Donor of the Year Banquet. Honoring the Estate of Rebekah Cohen Wentworth.*

Inside, a hotel ballroom like any other: straight tracks ran along the ceiling, ready to extrude opaque sheets of sound-baffling, quick-setting gel. The gel was a poor cousin to the materials used in Gray's interrogation facilities in suburban New Jersey, but would easily block out the blather and spectacle of a wedding reception behind the walls. The ballroom waited in banquet mode, round tables covered in smooth white linen and service for eight. Podium at the far end. Bar to the left. A quick scan by eye, confirmed by his implantable, counted nineteen people mingled between the bar and the tables.

Stone's mother did a quick scan too, with a minimal angle of her head and eyes. She disengaged from his arm. "Be a dear and get me a cosmopolitan," she said, and strode off before he could reply.

Seventy-five years old and still on the prowl. The wonders of rejuvenation tech. Stone shook his head with a wry grin and went to the bar.

A few taps on an ordering tablet set the robot arms into motion. Ice clattered against stainless steel. Liquids poured. Seconds later, he set out, the stem of his mother's cosmopolitan in his right hand and a glass of sparkling water in his left.

"So you're Sheila Chalmers," boomed a raspy male voice. "You must be proud of your grandmother's work."

Stone drew closer. A tall man looking somewhere in middle age, with kinked black hair and a trimmed beard covering a pointed jaw. Gold threads edged the pocket square festooning his four-button silk jacket. Handsome and rich enough to get his mother's attention, now that she was between boyfriends.

"I'm deeply honored her books still speak to audiences a century later," Stone's mother said. "And I'm delighted to donate the proceeds to the Society. I don't need the money, and she would have wanted her religious community to benefit." Her voice lilted but her body language was off. She had an agenda beyond flirting with the tall man.

She took her drink, then turned and extended an arm toward a younger woman to the tall man's side. The gesture explained her body language. "Daniel and Rachel Featherington, this is my son, Rolston."

Featherington didn't sound like a Jewish name. But, hell, neither did *Wentworth*. A firm handshake with Daniel. "Call me Stone."

"Stone? How'd you come by a nickname like that?"

"I fall on things from a great height and crush them." Stone turned to Rachel. Strawberry blond hair rose in a fountain from her head, and her pointy chin confirmed a family resemblance, that Featherington was her father and not husband. Freckles dusted her cheeks. Her hand lingered in his while her blue eyes regarded him. A delicate floral perfume reached his nose, one of those custom formulations based on pheromones and the wearer's genomic data, designed to go through a man's nose straight to his brain.

Thanks to Gray's training, Stone could resist her perfume. If he wanted.

"I've long admired your great-grandmother's books," Rachel said.

"They really empowered me to shake off patriarchy and embrace female sexual expression as a *tikkun olam*." Gaze intent, she withdrew her hand, sliding smooth skin over his.

A ticking—? His implantable popped a subtitle into his vision. *Repair of the world.*

He put on a lazy smile and matched her gaze. "Female sexuality has certainly made my world a better place."

Yet as he said the words, a weary feeling tugged down his mood. Yet another social event, yet another attractive woman, yet another hookup, yet another name forgotten the next morning.

Not that he had anything better to do tonight. A plan formed in his subconscious. Get her away from her father and his mother, tease her about the WASP in the woodpile who provided her family name, then—.

Rachel smiled coyly, then touched his arm. "What's your line of work, Stone?"

He gestured with his sparkling water, aiming toward the Upper East Side. "I'm a consultant for a UN agency."

"Consultant? That means you travel to exotic places?"

And kill people. He shrugged. "You transit one wormhole, you've transited them all."

Stone took a sip of sparkling water when a ding sounded in his ear. Between him and Rachel's pale, freckled cheeks, bright green text appeared in midair. *Come to office immediately. A 487 on Trinity. Out.*

Gray. No one else could force messages through his wearable.

Stone let out a breath. "Speaking of which, duty calls."

"You have to leave?" Rachel asked. Her lips formed a faint pout. "Surely it can wait till tomorrow?"

"Wish it could. Pardon me." He withdrew a step and faced his mother.

After a moment, she broke away from Featherington. A scowl formed on her face. "You're leaving?"

"A problem at work. I'll tell my car to come back for you."

His mother shook her head, eyelids heavy with disapproval. "Stone—"

"Don't worry about it, Sheila," said Featherington. "I'll make sure you get home after the banquet. He needs to go. Taking care of UN business is a *tikkun olam* of its own."

Featherington's words hung around Stone's mind as he strode through the hotel's atrium. Repair the world? Stone lashed humankind's parts together to keep them from flying off—or bulleting into the engine that kept the world turning. The saddle-shaped after-image of the memorial came to his mind's eye. Seventy years ago, the terrorists almost succeeded in crippling that engine. Never again.

Five minutes later, Stone nestled in the back seat and his coupe accelerated through the nest of ramps from Pearl onto the FDR north-bound. "Override code," he said.

On the highway, Stone's coupe accelerated further, slipped around cars driving the speed limit. He shut his eyes and mulled the call. 487. Grand theft. Grand theft? What item stolen on some backwater world could be important enough for Gray to summon him?

UN headquarters soon came into view, its straight lines and flat faces of white marble and blue-green glass distinctive against the curved, nanotube black residential highrises behind it. The setting sun threw gray shadows interspersed with slivers of daylight halfway across the East River.

Minutes later, UN headquarters loomed above the FDR, as large as it looked in a million worldforum posts describing the tireless work of the Secretary-General and the ambassador corps in maintaining harmony between the teeming billions on Earth and the colony worlds. Stone raised the back of his hand to cover a yawn. His coupe took the 42nd Street exit for the UN's real center of power.

UNICA headquarters looked like any other of the thousand office buildings housing the government of mankind. The eighty-story building occupied half a block in the mid 50's east of Lexington Avenue. Pedestrians in the costume of a dozen UN member states weaved between the concrete bollards and angled steel bolted to the sidewalk and securing the facility from truck bombs. The sign between the parking garage's entrance and exit showed four multiracial hands clasped together over the UN flag, with subtle text reading *United Nations Interagency Coordination Authority*.

Stone's coupe pulled into the garage and stopped near the elevator lobby. He climbed out and his coupe drove away even before the lobby swung its doors open for him.

Minutes later he emerged from the elevator on the 27th floor, and crossed plush tan carpet to Gray's office.

Gray sat near the window at a round table holding a tablet computer and a glass of whisky. Late in the evening on a hot summer day, he still looked cool and crisp, hair swept back and holding its place, the knot in his blue silk tie tight against his collar. He glanced up from the tablet, his eyes like polished granite, meeting Stone's gaze before looking toward the drink table in the far corner. "Pour yourself a sparkling water and take a seat." He nodded toward the other chair at the round table.

Stone cracked open a bottle. He carried a fizzing glass by his fingertips around the rim toward Gray. With a faint hum of its electric motor, the empty chair rolled a foot away from the table to give him room to sit.

"I trust your mother wasn't offended I called away her date to the banquet," Gray said.

Stone waved his fingers. "There were rich and single men there."

"No doubt rich and single women, as well." Gray lifted his glass. His whisky smelled of sea air and damp earth. He peered down his long, narrow nose and said, "I suspect the answer will be 'not much,' but what can you tell me about the planet Trinity?"

"I assume the founders were Christians, probably from the USA."

Gray raised an eyebrow.

"Don't be so shocked. I may not have a god, but there's a church with Trinity in its name a few blocks from my apartment."

"Not that. What makes you say the founders were from the US?"

Stone shrugged. "During the Time of Troubles, only the USA had enough Christians who could afford the price of transit with the rogue warpdrive ships. Am I wrong?"

"You guessed well. What's happened on Trinity since its founding?"

"It was the twelfth or so, maybe fifteenth, colony to accede to the Dubai Convention. Twenty-five years ago. The terrestrial end of the wormhole is in the Republic of Sarawak."

Gray raised his eyebrows. "I hadn't expected you to remember that."

"Maybe I overheard a conversation when I changed planes in Singapore a few years ago."

"I see. Anything more?"

Stone sipped water tasting thickly of minerals. "Trinity acceded long enough ago for resettled from Earth to outnumber the founding population by, what, ten-to-one?"

"In fact, the ratio is now about sixteen-to-one, with most resettled coming from the Free State of Shenzen and a smattering of African countries."

A million Chinese and Africans, undesired by their home governments, dumped on sixty thousand colonists who'd forgotten why their ancestors fled Earth in the first place. "Any more background I need?"

"You'll probably forget this before you transit the wormhole. Trinity is a tidally-locked moon of a gas giant named Bethany. Trinity has an extremely dense, breathable atmosphere. The native photosynthetic lifeforms have emerged from the oceans within the past hundred million years and are slowly spreading like moss and fungus across Trinity's lower altitudes. The colony settled on and is limited to a plateau about eight thousand meters above Trinity's sea level."

"I almost never say you're wrong, but here's one time."

"Oh?"

"I'll forget all that before I leave for the wormhole." Stone shook his head, then swept his smirk off his face. "Your call said a 487. Who stole what from whom?"

"We don't know who. The whom is the UN Office of Advanced Industrial and Manufacturing Assistance Services."

Stone squinted. The UN agency name meant nothing. Ten thousand bureaucrats in a skyscraper a few blocks away, touching files and lobbying for bigger budgets. "Refresh my memory on UN-O-A-I—"

"Its preferred acronym is UNAIM. 'Advanced industry and manufacturing' means molecular fabrication—nanoscale 3d printing and the like."

"And the what?" Stone loosened his necktie's knot. The answer hit him. "Someone hacked into UNAIM's servers on Trinity and copied over weapons plans." Stone imagined the harm Teresa Benavides could have worked on Freeland with better weapons, and shivered. Ice cubes clinked against his glass. He set down his drink. "Why would UNAIM store weapons plans on a colony world? We wouldn't allow the locals to fab weap—"

"UNAIM doesn't do that." More disapproval than usual laced Gray's voice.

"Officially."

"Our field office on Trinity report no evidence that UNAIM—or rogue UNAIM employees—have done it unofficially, either."

"Okay, not weapons…. What plans could be worth copying over, then?"

Gray lifted his whisky glass halfway to his mouth. "UNAIM's servers on Trinity contain plans for fusion reactors, drive nozzles, and pressurized hulls."

"Spaceship parts."

"Precisely."

Stone pressed his lips together. "But not warpdrive ship tech. The most the thieves could build is a slower-than-light spaceship. Even if the thieves build one, they would need a decade to reach even a nearby system. A century, more, probably, to reach Earth." He drank sparkling water, smiled. "Look, I'm glad you called me away from that banquet, but sending me to investigate the theft of plans for an inter-planetary ship is overkill."

Gray sipped whisky, then turned his cold eyes on Stone. "This mission requires your talents. Our partners will explain why."

CHAPTER 2

The restaurant filled the uppermost floor of a skyscraper in the mid-40's with shades of black and white. Waiters in dark jackets and bow ties paced silently around tables draped by starched and ironed linen, pouring deep red wine and setting out plates of vat-grown ivory. Women wore black dresses and dangling pearl earrings, and shades of gray suited the men. In a corner, a dark cylindrical hologram surrounded a table like a thick curtain, rippling and shimmering. Outside the windows, office and residential lights glowed in the surrounding highrises against the gray, light-polluted evening.

The restaurant's brightest splash of color came from Caitlyn Fredriksen's hazel eyes.

Stone kept his stride between tables steady and his usual look of detached amusement on his face. *Why her?* he subvoked to Gray through his implantable.

You worked well with her on Freeland, Gray subvoked back. *Yes?* The flesh-colored sensor pad on the side of his adam's apple flexed with the faint motions of his throat muscles. An archaic interface, but who could command him to upgrade?

I did. Young, a little squeamish at up-close wetwork, but competent —for a keyhole kop. *But I work better alone.*

Gray ignored him and leaned toward the only other person seated at Caitlyn's table, to her right. "Mr. Holbrook, how do you do?" Gray extended his hand.

Stone took note of Holbrook with a single glance. A bald scalp jutted above a crown of reddish-brown hair. His shoulders and torso, wide and soft, suggested he'd been muscular in his younger days. A frosted mug of dark beer sat in front of him, a sign he would get wider and softer. No telling his formal rank inside the UN's Interstellar Transport Bureau—ITB—but, informally at least, he might be almost as powerful as Gray.

"Just fine, Mr. Gray. Glad to match a face to the name and voice." Holbrook spoke from a narrow mouth buried behind a mustache and gray-flecked beard. He turned pale blue eyes at Stone. "Mr. Chalmers?"

"Stone will do."

"Oh, I'm sure it will. Caitlyn tells me you did good work on Freeland."

"Most of it with her help." Stone smirked at her.

Caitlyn folded her arms and arched an eyebrow at Holbrook. "Sit, please," Holbrook said.

Stone sat to Caitlyn's left. For a moment, he took in her blond waterfall of hair spilling over her shoulders. Their mission together had been purely professional, and he never mixed business with plea-sure—but she was easy on the eyes and old habits died hard. "You didn't get enough of me on Freeland?" he asked.

"This isn't my idea. I don't want a partner in this. Do you?"

"No. But you're one up on me."

She quirked an eyebrow. "How so?"

"You know what *this* is."

She took her hand from the stem of her white wine glass, raised one slender finger to her lips. Her hazel gaze darted to Holbrook.

Holbrook minimally dipped his chin. A dark, incurving wall snapped into view behind them. The holocurtain would prevent anyone outside their table from reading lips, but it wouldn't stop sound waves. Time to subvoke.

Stone sat up straighter and nodded, his face set in a businesslike expression. Unlike Gray's briefings, Holbrook might say something that could help Stone stay alive on this mission.

Holbrook subvoked, *Stone, I'm now going to tell you something highly classified and extremely secret. I greatly deviated from ITB policy in making Mr. Gray aware of it. The Secretary-General himself doesn't even know it.*

I'm listening.

Holbrook's pale blue gaze drilled into Stone's eyes. *One of the rogue warpdrive ships from the Time of Troubles is unaccounted for.*

Stone blinked, once. From the corner of his eye, Caitlyn's gaze on his face was a hot, live thing.

A thousand disasters had struck Earth in the Time of Troubles, the middle decades of the twenty-first century. The atomic bomb that killed Stone's great-grandmother and a quarter-million other people in lower Manhattan had been just one. Reestablishing order occupied the power brokers in New York, Washington, Silicon Valley, London, Tokyo, and Berlin for twenty years. While they glued the bottle together and shoved the genie back in, a libertarian billionaire and a team of aspergery physicists and semi-autonomous robots escaped the UN's reach. The billionaire's team built a factory at the Sun-Venus L4 point, where a million square kilometers of solar panels powered the production of space-warping exotic matter.

Worse, the billionaire sold his exotic matter to anyone with an airtight can and a fusion reactor open at one end. The rogue ships then offered transit to any group of fanatics who wanted to flee Earth and spend weeks or months accelerating down a tunnel of warped space to an interstellar planet inhabitable by humans.

Turning the galaxy into the breeding ground for a second Time of Troubles.

After the power brokers restored stability on Earth, at the price of a thousand destroyed cities and five billion dead, they turned their sights on the libertarian billionaire. From time to time, after a third glass of Scotch, Gray hinted he knew the full story. Whatever the truth, the billionaire was dead. ITB administered the exotic matter factory—renamed Hawking Station—and monopolized its products. First, a fleet of warships, built for the hunt. All the rogue pilots lay dead in spaceport bars or floated bug-eyed and blood-boiled in warpdrive ships holed and vented to vacuum. ITB's salvage crews melted down the alloys and carved up the hull plates of the last rogue warpdrive ship decades ago.

Stone covered a yawn with a sip of sparkling water. The powers that be lied. So what?

Enough to lead Gray to collaborate with the head keyhole kop. *Maybe I'm missing the big picture,* Stone said. *How much harm could one warpdrive ship cause?*

Under his balding pate, Holbrook's blue eyes peered at Stone. *You know about the meteor impact that annihiliated the dinosaurs? Left a crater a hundred miles across under the present-day Yucatan peninsula?*

I'll take your word for it.

A warpdrive ship at high speed could strike Earth with ten times more energy than that. If the pilot aimed at Central Park, his ship's impact would vaporize everything from Philadelphia to Boston. The shockwave would crumble every building in the US and Canada. Then airborne dust would blot out sunlight for a decade. Worldwide.

A heavy silence settled on them, broken when Gray rested his whisky glass on the pale linen. *Even if no pilot were suicidal enough to implement Holbrook's doomsday scenario, a warpdrive ship in the wrong hands could cause vast damage to the UN's position in the galaxy. A colony could use it to attack an ITB mission towing a wormhole out from Earth, or to shuttle soldiers or military equipment to interfere with UN activities on a Dubai Convention world. A sufficiently advanced colony could even reverse engineer the warpdrive in a bid to understand exotic matter technology and build a fleet of such ships. In that circumstance, such a colony could conceivably attack and conquer Earth.*

Behind Stone, a man cleared his throat. Holbrook raised his hand. Stone and the others nodded. The rippling holographic wall vanished, revealing a waiter with a long, narrow nose and fleshy earlobes. The lines of his face mapped out a decades-long career spent catering to the rich and powerful in this room. "Lady, gentlemen, your orders?"

While Caitlyn ordered a second glass of wine and a spinach salad with seared tuna, a lazy smile formed on Stone's lips. The world could be devastated tomorrow and this waiter—all the business and government leaders around them—hell, all the city's twenty million people—had no idea. Only the four of them at the table had any clue. "Tonic with lime. T-bone, medium rare. Roasted brussels sprouts. Baked potato, all the way." A fitting meal before going off to save the world.

After the waiter took Gray and Holbrook's orders, the holocurtain blinked back into place.

Stone subvoked first. *Mr. Holbrook, my guess is you think the missing warpdrive ship is somewhere in Trinity system.*

Holbrook slid his beer mug to the side, then focused on Stone. *My researchers have narrowed down its location to a short list of candidates, and Trinity's stellar system is high on it.*

Except ITB hasn't detected it in the twenty-five years you've been on Trinity.

On is the keyword. Our initial scout mission and the subsequent wormhole transport expedition were the only times we've had assets above Trinity's atmosphere. Both the scouts and the wormhole tugs followed standard procedures. As they approached and departed Trinity, they looked for gravitational distortions caused by a warpdrive in action. They also scanned for metallic objects orbiting the suns, planets, or moons, as well as the waste heat signatures of a fusion reactor. If a ship shut down its warpdrive and reactor, and rocky or icy material camouflaged it, the scanners wouldn't find it.

A brief, wry smile flexed Holbrook's red mustache and beard. *Turns out the tugs' scans did pick up a slight heat anomaly, which my predecessors overlooked at the time. Consistent with a fusion reactor operating in a caretaker mode. Powering a ship's internal systems, but not enough for interplanetary travel or warpdrive.*

Stone frowned. He glanced at Gray, who in response raised an eyebrow two millimeters. Go ahead and ask, Stone read. To Holbrook, Stone asked, *Why do you need us? Haven't you already sent a scout ship to investigate the anomaly?*

If it were up to me, I would have sent a scout to Trinity a year ago. Unfortunately, there are bureaucrats above me on ITB's org chart whom I haven't politicked into approving the mission. Holbrook tossed back a long swallow of beer. *And if you're wondering why I won't wait, the risks of a rogue warpdrive ship are too immense for me to go it alone.*

Gray enveloped his whisky glass with long fingers. *Holbrook came to me four months ago and impressed me with the need to cooperate in this matter. I promised him I would share with him any intel indicating the unaccounted warpdrive ship might be brought into play.*

And we agreed to joint action if he did, Holbrook added.

Stone glanced at Caitlyn. Shrugged.

I still don't see the need for Stone and I to work together. Caitlyn's voice rang in his mind's ear like an ambulance siren a few blocks away. She leaned toward Holbrook. *You know I'm capable—*

And I'm more capable, Stone added, giving Holbrook a lazy smile.

In the corner of Stone's eye, Gray minimally shook his head. *Not capable enough.*

Damned right, Holbrook said. He glanced at Caitlyn. *That goes for both of you. This project lies beyond your individual skill sets.* His blue eyes blazed from his ruddy face. *Stone, I'll cover your dinner out of my own pocket, forget the expense account, if you can prove to me you're Caitlyn's equal in exotic matter physics.*

Stone matched Holbrook's gaze. *I can speedlearn it.*

Holbrook shook his head and sloshed from side to side his mug of dark beer. *It would take too long to get you to the level of warpdrive engineering we need on this team. Caitlyn's starting from a higher base. She'll speedlearn it.*

You'll be too occupied, Gray said to Stone, *hypnogoguing the skills to pilot an interplanetary fusion-propulsion vessel.*

Holbrook raised russet eyebrows at Caitlyn. *Because he's starting from a higher base.*

She sniffed in a breath. Holbrook went on. *I read your report, and his, about Freeland, as well as his dossier from Gray. He's a better driver and pilot than you are. We need each of you to set aside your egos and maximize your strengths.*

You left out firearms, Stone said.

Caitlyn pressed her lips together. Her large hazel eyes glinted. *I can certainly set aside my ego. Stone's ego speaks for itself.*

Stone chuckled, then turned his shoulders away from her, toward

Gray. *I'm going to speedlearn interplanetary piloting skills? The idea being I find the thieves, get accepted into their group, and offer to fly a ship they cobbled together out of stolen plans to the missing warpdrive ship?*

Precisely. Fly the ship to Earth if possible; otherwise, destroy its warpdrive capability.

Only one problem. *And the thieves are—?*

Gray's lips compressed for a moment. *We have several separatist groups on Trinity under surveillance, but no hard evidence that any of them were behind this. I'll transmit the reports to you. Read them. When you arrive on Trinity, visit our field office for an update. In case the perpetrators or Trinity's government know about our field office and keep it under surveillance, you can enter unseen from a UN cultural affairs office on a different floor of the building.*

An icy sensation sliced down behind Stone's right eye. He drank sparkling water to mask any tell, then switched to a private connection. *Sneaking in won't help us if a UN employee—or a UNICA employee—provides intel to the thieves or Trinity's government.* He looked intently at a spot on the tablecloth in front of him.

We have no evidence of espionage against us, in contrast to Freeland. And none of the UN employees on the list of potential security risks from Freeland are employed on Trinity. Enough, our collaborators want—

Back on the connection shared by the four of them, Holbrook said, *You should also mention....*

Indeed, Gray said. *In addition to your skills, you two will also both hypnogogue personas for your cover stories.*

Stone shrugged. Caitlyn angled her head toward Holbrook. *What?*

His people are better at generating cover stories than we are. Holbrook drank from his mug, his blue eyes fixed on her face.

On Freeland I saw through Stone's—

Holbrook's mug thumped on the table. *Because you knew who he really was. His cover story fooled Lukas and Theresa Benavides, didn't it? Our usual trick of pretending you're a harmless UN employee won't cut it.*

From nearby came the aromas of a sizzling steak and the pungent, garlicky scent of brussels sprouts. The waiter cleared his throat again. Holbrook raised his eyebrow and looked a question to each of the others. Gray nodded. An instant later, the holocurtain vanished.

Stone's eyes needed a fraction of a second to refocus on the view out the windows. Not as young as he once was. Bah, a trip to the rejuvenation clinic would fix him.

The waiter placed Stone's plate. A seared brown steak, reddish-pink inside, and shredded shades of green interspersed with translucent slivers of garlic. He reached for his fork and knife. His stomach rumbled with anticipation.

"Bon appetit," Gray said. It seemed odd to hear his voice coming from his mouth after the recent minutes of subvoking and transcranial stim hitting their auditory nerves.

Holbrook nodded. "Enjoy your meals." *You're booked on the six a.m. suborbital from Kennedy to Singapore.*

CHAPTER 3

An hour later, while the UNICA tower slumbered, Stone rode up the elevator to the 29th floor. Half the overhead lights were off in the hallways. A janitor—frizzy black hair, copper-brown face, stiff blue uniform—stepped to the side. "Shoo, shoo," he said as he waved his cleaning robots, terrier-sized centaurs, out of Stone's way. He spoke in a thick accent Stone couldn't place. "Good evening, sir."

"Evening." A simple word, but how many spy agencies had been dealt low by a disgruntled low-level employee? A polite word might keep a custodian in his place more than a thousand hidden cams and mics. Stone accented the word with a crisp nod, then continued on.

He rounded a corner. Grinding electric guitars, thumping drums, and galloping electric bass trickled from an ajar door labeled *Operational Support*.

The corners of Stone's mouth lifted. Century-old—or older?—heavy metal music could only mean Jürgen worked in cover stories tonight. Stone rapped his knuckles on the ajar door, then pushed it wide open.

A sand-colored counter of cultured stone separated a waiting area near the door from a gray farm of cubicles receding around a corner of the L-shaped room. Jürgen stood with one elbow on the counter, his chin resting on his elevated hand, his fingers tapping his cheek and his long head bobbing with the main rhythm of the drums. His hooded blue eyes flicked up and he lifted his head. "Hybrid. Good evening."

Years earlier, Stone took the codename *Hybrid* from his variegated great-grandparents—an NFL cornerback; Rebekah Cohen Wentworth, the rabbi who claimed God wanted women to be sluts; a Mexican-American television journalist from whom he inherited his blond hair. Inside the office, only Gray knew, and used, *Stone*. "Good to see you. Do you ha—?"

Jürgen reached under the counter and rested two stacked transparent folios in front of Stone. "Yes."

"I appreciate how well you do your job." He palmed the uppermost folio and slid it off the other to the right. The folio under his hand held a manilla envelope as blue as a summer afternoon's sky. Inside the other folio, a fluorescent pink envelope made him squint. "Kind of clichéd, don't you think?"

"My team worked hard to prepare a male and a female cover story. Please don't cross them up."

"Your team? You didn't work on it yourself?"

Jürgen slid his hand down his cheek while giving Stone a jaundiced look. "Every persona you've ever gotten from us has been a team effort. Including the Jezhek persona you used on Freeland that you think Fabrizio fouled up."

"That one was damn-all intrusive. You read my report, didn't you? Ran your diagnostics?"

Jürgen rolled his wrists in a hand-shrug. "We're continually refining our processes. Sometimes our refinements don't work as we intend. We erred and corrected it. These two personas won't interfere with your mission."

Stone mulled the other's words. Jürgen was good at his job—good enough to push back to Gray if a field operative made arrogant requests about who should code up which personas. "That's all I can ask for. Thanks for staying late to hand them to me yourself."

"Use them wisely."

Stone unzipped the folios and slid out the envelopes. They even felt different—the pink envelope with the female persona felt smooth to the touch, from plastic coated or woven into the paper, far more slick than the heavy texture of the blue. The envelopes' contents felt similar —small objects of hard metal, one round, one linear, along with a rigid plastic cylinder. He would examine them later.

Each folio also held a plastic object the same color as its envelope. Each object was the size of the last joint of his little finger with a clip on the back. Standard issue.

"Don't I always?" he said with a grin.

Jürgen's blue eyes remained hooded. "You've made it home in one piece after every mission. That's not the same thing. Good evening, Hybrid." He turned and shambled into the cubicle farm in the depths of the room.

Grumbling techs kept the galaxy together. Stone chuckled to himself and left for the elevators.

Fifteen minutes later, he padded into his apartment and quietly locked the door behind him. Even so, the clack of the deadbolt into its hole echoed off the undecorated wallboard and bare glass of the windows, momentarily overcoming the low hum of the air conditioning. His eyes adjusted to the gray light cast by a thousand highrises on the dark, rectilinear couches and tables in his living room. A faint sound came from the kitchen—orchestral bombast and fat ladies singing. Old Mr. Leipziger in the next apartment listened to opera again.

Gray light and his spatial awareness led Stone to his bedroom. The opera faded out of hearing and a warm, serene feeling told him his implantable would wake him in time for his flight. He shucked his shoes and jacket, stropped his tie out from under his collar, tossed dress shirt and pants to the robotic wheeled hamper synced with his dry cleaning and laundry service. Five minutes later he was asleep.

He woke at 3:30, eyes still gritty. *I need clothes for the environment near Trinity's wormhole mouth,* he subvoked to his implantable. Though if he piloted a hacked-together ship across Trinity's system, no telling what kind of climate control he might have on board. *And a pair of exercise shorts and a winter coat.*

Two bulbs in the closet cast double smears of reflections on the windows, set to matte-black for privacy. Panels the full depth of the closet defined eight cubbies stretching from floor to ceiling. In each cubby, a shirt and pair of pants hung from a bar and brushed the top of a carryon roller case. One bulb shone in the ceiling of the left-most cubby. Another glowed in the cubby furthest to the right.

From the cubby on the left, he pulled the roller case and flung it to the bed. Stone traced his fingers along the seam in the roller case and its lid swung up. He stepped into thin pants of khaki linen, found a short sleeve shirt of the same material but black and thicker. Before he put on the shirt, he found his waistband holster and dabbed the back of the straps and pocket with anti-chafe cream. From the firearm safe under his bed he retrieved his .357 pistol, slid it into the holster, snapped the flap closed. The holster clipped inside his waistband at the small of his back. The untucked tail of his shirt concealed it further. He didn't need to look in the mirror to know the pistol made a negligible print under his clothing.

He reached back into the firearm safe. Two magazines of cartridges went into zippered pockets in his pants, and a compact 9 mm slid into an ankle holster strapped to the inside of his left leg.

A winter coat and long, thermal pants and shirt barely fit with the other garments in the roller case. Stone laid the pink and blue envelopes on top of the coat and flopped the lid down. While the lid resealed itself, he stepped into brown hiking shoes with flexible treaded soles and breathable uppers and drank half a glass of water. His mouth felt less cottony. Though still sluggish, his thoughts flowed now like a thawing river. His mind would unlimber in good time. Hours of travel remained before he had a chance to save the world.

Ten minutes later, his black coupe descended the ramp to the Midtown Tunnel. Even at this hour, pole-mounted highway lights shone down on a steady pulse of boxy cars and delivery trucks plying the Long Island Expressway and the Van Wyck south across Queens. Queens? He squinted to make sure the cars had passengers. Sure enough, people inside. What could lead someone to drive across Queens at four in the morning? Stone frowned. A job?

He shook his head. Poor bastards. Leading lives of quiet desperation? How many of them would welcome a rogue warpdrive ship slamming into the city at nearly the speed of light, freeing them from their pointless lives?

Pointless? As if his wasn't?

The hell? *Get some more sleep*, he told himself, then shut his eyes.

After a few drowsy minutes, his coupe slowed and took a ramp. His body senses told him where he was before he opened his eyes. Double-parked cars brushed bumpers in front of a long building of glass panels and straight, metallic lines. Sixty years old, in the rectilinear, retro twentieth-century style of UN headquarters, everyone called it the new international terminal.

His black coupe wedged into a spot, popped its trunk and doors. Muggy air bore the stink of overworked electric motors. Brakes squeaked and skycaps manhandled suitcases onto their robotic carts. The roller wheels on Stone's carryon ticked over seams in the concrete as he wound through the maze of parked cars to the doors. His car pulled away for the journey back to his building, where it would wait for his implantable to summon it when his suborbital return flight approached JFK.

The glass panels and interior walls of the terminal concentrated cool air and the chatter of a hundred conversations. Caitlyn waited outside the security queue. Her fingers rested on the extended handle of her rolling suitcase. Her mouth formed a tight line and her forehead glowed with sweat. No wonder—she wore a tan jacket over an untucked, heather-green blouse. A pistol in a shoulder holster slightly distorted the lines of her jacket.

He glanced at her hidden pistol just long enough for her to realize she saw it, then looked up. "It's pretty obvious," he murmured.

A TSA security policeman trotted by, both hands on a submachinegun held by a loop around his neck. Caitlyn pressed her lips more tightly together. She muttered, "We don't transport—such items —on our persons on civilian flights."

Stone lifted his left hand over his mouth and yawned. "The flight manifest lists you and me as UN air marshals. Do you think Gray's an idiot?"

"No, but…. What if a situation arises that requires an air marshal?"

"Then we play the role. It's easier than being a keyhole kop."

"Are you going to insult me the entire trip?"

He angled his head toward the pre-screened first-class security line. "Follow me." He started off. From the slap of her soles and the rattle of her suitcase's wheels, she hurried to catch up.

"Trust me," she said around her breaths, "I see through your alpha game nonsense."

He shrugged, a smirk on his face. "You're following me, aren't you?"

They entered the security line. Back and forth through hairpin turns defined by retractable black cord. Stone went first through the checkpoint. Roller case on the conveyor for the X-ray. Thumbprint and retina scan for identification. Inside the body scanner, he put his hands on his head. The untucked tail of his shirt rose, but remained below his waistband, hiding his .357.

A dark-skinned woman whose headscarf color-matched her blue TSA uniform watched a monitor. She gasped. She turned wide eyes to Stone. "Oh, sir, do dome on through," she said in a French accent.

Stone smiled at her, then twisted the smile into a smirk at Caitlyn.

Caitlyn straightened her back and flashed a glare from her hazel eyes. Her anger got her through security without a second glance from the TSA employee.

After clearing security, Caitlyn strode alongside Stone, her face as cold and craggy as an alpine peak. The crowd gabbed in dozens of languages. Bleary-eyed business travelers lined up at the coffee bar. Stone winced at the scent of fresh grounds. Only fools needed stimulants to perk themselves up. Down the concourse from the hiss of milk frothers, they passed a bank of shoeshine boxes, where dandified young men wearing waxed mustaches and flowers in their lapels shoved black, synthetic leather wingtips into the boxes' robotic maws.

Stone stopped at a robot-tended gift shop. "Two bottles of water," he said, and robot arms snaked from behind the counter to a chiller case. Stone took the bottles and handed one to Caitlyn. "You'll be thirsty once we're on board."

At their gate, the suborbital waited at the end of the jetway. Under the rear section of the long, skinny passenger compartment, men guided flexible robotic fuel lines, erupting from the tarmac like blind worms, to the nozzles on the suborbital's hydrogen tanks.

The forty passengers boarded in one group—on a suborbital, every ticket was first-class—down a center aisle between rows of two seats per side. Caitlyn took the window seat while Stone slid the pink and blue envelopes out of his roller case, along with two black eyemasks and a tube of earplugs. After stowing both their cases in the overhead, he handed her the pink envelope and the matching plastic object from his pocket, then sat.

Clip that— He pointed at the small plastic object. *—onto your blouse near your implantable. Like this.* He shoved his hand into his pocket, emerged with the blue object, and squeezed to open the clip. He reached in through his collar and clipped the blue plastic item to his shirt over his chest.

Caitlyn did so without complaint. Good; she understood UNICA was more advanced at cover stories than ITB, and she wasn't going to argue.

Reach into the envelope for your medicine.

She opened the pink envelope and turned its gaping mouth toward her gaze.

He popped his fingernail against the pink envelope. *Don't look at what's inside. Speedlearn your cover story persona first.*

She reached in for a pharmacy bottle. Red-brown plastic, white lid. She peered at the fake name on the label. *Looks completely realistic. Good attention to detail.* She raised an eyebrow at him. *I conclude you had nothing to do with it.*

Stone gave her a jaundiced look. He pulled her water bottle from her seat pocket. *There are two tablets and a capsule inside. The order is green, yellow, red. Wait at least five seconds between each, and recap the water bottle as soon as you take the red. Repeat it back to me.*

Caitlyn repeated the instructions in a grudging tone. *How does this work?*

The drugs knock you out and render your brain susceptible to the persona data in the clip-on. Your implantable will use transcranial stim to insert the persona into your brain.

She still looked hesitant.

If you need to know the neuro-physio mechanism of each drug, I can't help you.

"Okay," she said aloud. She looked at the pharmacy bottle in her hand. "Start now?"

"Now."

Caitlyn downed the green while he retrieved his speedlearning dose from the blue envelope. He took the green while she took her yellow. She popped the red and hesitated a moment before recapping the bottle. Her fingers fumbled and a moment of surprise jolted her hazel eyes wide. He took her hand in his and recapped the bottle for her.

"Thanks," she muttered. Her eyes slid shut and her torso slumped against the backrest.

Stone took the yellow tablet, sloughed out a breath. He'd been timid the first time he'd speedlearned a persona, too. He dropped the red capsule on his tongue, chased it with water, immediately capped the bottle.

Within seconds he joined her in unconsciousness. Their speedlearning programs started before the suborbital reached the end of the taxiway.

CHAPTER 4

A convulsive gasp for air woke both of him.

A blonde sat next to him, her long hair matted with sweat, her hazel eyes wide, her mouth open, and rapid shallow breaths pumping her torso. Behind her, the rounded black square of an aircraft window.

His wife, but what were they doing on a plane?

His wife?

"Sweetheart," he said, his voice odd. He cleared his throat. "Angela."

Angela?

Caitlyn?

She gasped again. This time it took. Her torso ballooned with a deep inhalation. Caitlyn leaned her head against the leather backrest and covered her eyes with her fingers. "What's happening?"

Caitlyn. And Angela. "There's a little disorientation," Stone said. "Your first time will be the worst."

"It's like I'm a suit that she put on...."

Angela, wife of Tobias Becker. They'd met at a small Christian university—such things still existed in the twenty-second century? Even in the rural Midwestern USA?—and worked two years as junior assistants at Hawking Station, before spending a dozen years as missionaries serving scattered settlements in the asteroid belt and the moons of Jupiter. During their flight, UNICA employees had created a data trail backing up their cover stories…

Empty facts. Stone uncapped his bottle and gulped lukewarm water.

Tobias Becker's memories welled at the floor of his mind, then gushed into place, trickling out to his fingertips. His first kiss with Angela, under the rustling leaves of a century-old oak on their college's campus. How had the speedlearning program spliced Caitlyn's face and figure into the persona's memories? Fingers nervously sliding forward the drive throttles during his first session in the cockpit simulator of an interplanetary ship. He and Angela fleeing in jetpacks through Thiel Colony's tunnels, muttering a prayer for forgiveness as he turned and aimed a rifle at the mob of neo-pagan libertarians. Under thrust, squeezing a bandage against the wound in Angela's belly, telling her all would be right if they trusted in the Lord. Telling her the same thing the next night, her tears floating through the cabin of their coasting ship as she sobbed about the miscarriage.

Caitlyn sucked in more shallow, rapid breaths. Her slender fingers pressed on her waistband, over the site of Angela Becker's wound. *No, that's… isn't it? Yes, my scar, from that wound I took on….*

Stone set his hand on her forearm. "You'll get over it." He switched to subvocal. *It's intense because the persona goes in deep. That means you don't have to think about it when you have to act in character.* His mouth felt clammy. No doubt hers felt worse. He pulled her water bottle from her seat pocket and opened it for her. "Here."

She reached both hands for the bottle, took a drink. She winced at the first mouthful, but swallowed it and chugged more. After handing the empty bottle to Stone, she dropped her hands to her lap.

"Better?"

"Better." She took a breath and said, *Whose idea was it our cover story should be a married couple?*

How sardonic is Holbrook's sense of humor?

Her brow crinkled for a moment. *Not very. Gray?*

Gray. He yawned, then twisted his forearm to bring his wristwatch into view. The watch automatically synced with local time. The platinum hands overlapped on the silicon wafer face, showing a few minutes before midnight. "We should be landing soon."

"My implantable says twenty-five minutes."

He nodded and reached for the blue envelope in the seat pocket. *Time to see what personal effects cover stories gave us.*

Stone unclasped the envelope. He reached in and his memory of how the objects pressed against the paper when he palmed them at UNICA headquarters told him what two of them were before he pulled them out. A wedding ring of plain gold. Delicate script ran around the inside. *Tobias and Angela. June 10, 2124. Eph. 5:25-28* Love, pride, humility, and piety all swirled inside the Tobias Becker persona.

He slid the ring down his finger and reached back inside the envelope. The linear objects were, of course, one item. He drew out a cross of pale, varnished wood, eyehooked to a steel chain. He looped the chain around his neck and tucked the cross inside his shirt. The cross clacked against the data clip, reminding him to remove the clip.

In the next seat, Caitlyn did the same. Her slender fingers closed the second button on her blouse, revealing a glimpse of her bra. He yawned again. Caitlyn was no more attractive than ten thousand other women in Manhattan, and long ago he'd taken *don't shit where you eat* to heart.

I'll take your clip, he said. She handed it over. With both her clip and his in his pocket, he went to the forward lavatory. His heel crushed both against the floor, and he flushed the fragments out of the suborbital twenty miles over southeast Asia. As he returned to his seat, the intercom bonged and the captain announced their descent.

A standard approach to Changi Airport. The skyscrapers of downtown Singapore lanced light toward the sky outside Caitlyn's window. Almost as impressive as the view of Manhattan from La Guardia. After landing, they made their way through concourses of gleaming chrome and backlit, translucent plastic, under the hard-eyed gaze of border policemen with semiautomatic rifles slung in front of their chests. Though crowds jammed Changi Airport even at midnight, brusque clerks efficiently routed them to the gate for their outgoing international flight, ninety minutes across the South China Sea to the Republic of Sarawak and the wormhole to Trinity.

Bumpy tropical air and glimmers of dawn woke Stone over the ocean. Jetlag and jumbled sleep turned the dark green mass of the island of Borneo into a dreamscape to the right of the plane. Descent made the terrain more solid, bringing into view the mouths of silty rivers and fringes of pale sand beach. A checkerboard of rice paddies and palm orchards ran from the shore toward the rainforest ten miles inland.

On the final approach to the local airport, Stone glimpsed a cargo ship with peeling paint tied up at a dock. Twenty Africans in green battle dress clutched assault rifles on the ship's top deck. The boxy shapes of armored personnel carriers waited along a rail line to the dock with machine guns and grenade launchers trained on the cargo ship. At a lager of jeeps, an obvious command center, drooped a pale blue UN flag.

The plane passed over a city of mid-rise buildings groaning under rooftop solar panels and signs in English and Chinese. A minute later, the wheels squealed on rough concrete.

Thick, hot air and the smells of roast pork and vinegar filled the cinder block terminal. A ceiling fan slowly turned above the border control kiosks. Stone and Caitlyn pressed thumbs and showed retinas to the biometric scanners. A Malay policeman in starched, short-sleeve khaki and a matching kepi hat peered at them, at a video monitor, back and forth. His finger, seemingly of its own will, smoothed his thin mustache. On a wall-filling mural behind the policeman, the glaring eyes of a grim, jowly Chinese man next to the gold, black, and red flag of the Republic of Sarawak. A founding father or the current president-for-life. Or both.

The policeman smoothed his mustache with an extra flourish, then scowled with beady eyes at Stone. He said in English, "You wear wedding rings."

Stone shifted his hand toward his wallet. "Yes."

"Yet your surnames differ."

Caitlyn's brows furrowed for a moment, then her face paled. The personas of the Becker couple existed only in her brain and Stone's, and in the effects hanging around their necks or snug on their ring fingers. The records presumably on the policeman's monitor showed them as Caitlyn Fredriksen and Rolston Chalmers.

"American custom allows each spouse to retain their surname," Stone said.

The policeman's eyebrow arched. "Is that so?"

"If our papers are in order," Caitlyn said, "please let us through. We have the wormhole train to catch."

The policeman's beady eyes swung to her. Stone groaned inwardly. *Now you've done it.* His fingertips entered his back pocket and touched worn leather.

"Your situation may require...." The policeman lifted his kepi and palmed black hair back from his brow. "...further consideration."

Caitlyn stiffened her back, jutted out her chin. "We're—"

"—quite appreciative of your hard work in a thankless job," Stone said. He pulled out his wallet and kept it below the kiosk's top. Out of sight of any anti-corruption cameras that might be hidden at the level of the founding father's eyes. From the wallet he drew two small denomination US banknotes, an Obama and a Clinton. A total of $6000, not enough to bother asking for a reimbursement from Gray—call it even after last night's steak dinner.

What the hell are you doing? Caitlyn subvoked. *We can play the air marshal card—*

He would still hold us while he checked. I thought we had a wormhole train to catch.

She scowled and looked away. Stone folded the two bills, palmed them, and rested both his hands on the edge of the kiosk. A corner of the Obama peeked out from under his hand, the green paper and multiple zeros apparent. "I'm sure you can overlook our odd American ways."

The policeman scowled more deeply, then leaned his upper body forward and slapped his hands on the kiosk a few inches from Stone's. "Do you think we are third world bigots who find your odd ways offensive?" The policeman's fingers crawled like spider legs toward Stone's hands. His forefinger stabbed down on the folded cash.

Stone raised his palm a fraction of an inch.

The policeman flexed his fingers and the folded bills disappeared. He stood taller and tapped a few softbuttons on his monitor. A light at the front of the kiosk glowed green. "Enjoy your travels through our country to the wormhole, Mrs. Fredriksen and Mr. Chalmers."

Stone led the way toward the ITB checkpoint at the train station. After they put twenty yards between them and the policeman, under an echoing metal ceiling and the hawking cries of vendors, she asked, "I take it you've studied reports on corruption in Southeast Asia?"

He laughed around a wry grin. "Don't you know me better than that?"

Her nostrils flared. "He could have thrown us in jail for trying to bribe him."

Stone switched to subvocal. *I've been in our line of work over fifteen years. I didn't need to study a desk jockey's report to know how he would react. How long have you been on the job?*

She jutted out her chin. *I've undertaken field work on seven different planets in three years.* Her hazel eyes dared him to laugh.

A smirk touched his lips and he patted her shoulder. *Then pay attention to me. You might learn something.* He leaned his roller case onto its wheels and turned his shoulders toward the ITB checkpoint.

What did I tell you about your alpha game nonsense? Her fist on her hip, Caitlyn's eyes flashed.

Time to nip her challenges in the bud. He dropped all smirkiness from his tone. *Look, it's obvious you want me to take you to bed.*

Don't flatter your—

I've got a firm don't-shit-where-you-eat policy. I've also got a dozen years and fifty missions on you. I've survived situations you wouldn't realize until too late might kill you. When I say you might learn something if you pay attention to me, I mean exactly that. He peered into her hazel eyes until she blinked her long lashes. *Now we have to catch the train to Trinity.*

Thanks to Gray and Holbrook's ability to feed false data into travel databases, the ITB clerks at the train station passed Tobias and Angela Becker without a second glance. Stone and Caitlyn would travel under their personas' names until they returned from Trinity. The only delay came in the departure lounge. Three hours. At least the swooping plastic chairs had plush cushioning.

Stone stretched his legs out and shut his eyes. His implantable fed maps and reports on Trinity's capital, Anderson City, and the UN facilities clustered along the train line between Anderson City and the wormhole. If Gray gave him that kind of facts, rather than tedious discussion of a planet's history and astronomy, he just might listen.

Late morning, a metallic hiss and squeal marked the arrival of the train. A green line appeared in his vision, tracing a path from the waiting room to the platform. A Sarawakan wearing a UN armband stowed their luggage while they boarded and took seats on the right side of the train's foremost passenger car. First class, or what passed for it in Sarawak: upholstered seats with rough stitching, and no robotic snack cart. A woman's smooth voice from the overhead speakers announced, in English and Malay, the train's impending departure.

The train lurched into motion, rolled slowly southwestward into the city. In crowded, blaring streets, mopeds and pedestrians slipped between slow-moving cars and trucks under the balconies of cheap apartment buildings. The wormhole lay a hundred miles inland, to the south.

Beyond the heart of the city, the train curved to the right. Sharp-edged quadrilaterals of morning sunlight expanded across the seats on the train car's left side.

"I thought the wormhole was to the south," Caitlyn said.

"It is."

"They why are we heading north?"

The old cargo ship at the dock, walled off by Sarawakan soldiers. "We're picking up passengers."

CHAPTER 5

A troubled look crossed Caitlyn's face. "Resettled?"

"Who else?"

She looked to the side, obviously checking data fed to her optic nerve by her implantable. "I can't tell if they're from Shenzen or the Organization of East African States?"

"From Africa," Stone said. "I saw their ship when we approached the airport. Don't worry, they won't ride with us."

"I know they have cars toward the back of the train. Will they get to sit, or will they be forced to stand?"

Stone shrugged and leaned his head back. He shifted over an inch to avoid a rough seam in the headrest. Eyes shut, he monitored the train's motion through his inner ear and the glow of daylight through his eyelids. Slowing, stopping, turning around. Tropical morning sunlight warmed his face. Backing toward the dock. A screeching whistle. A creak of brakes and the train stopped with a lurch.

Stone glanced out the window at a paved strip between the tracks and the water. An armored personnel carrier waited with a Sarawakan soldier at the opened top hatch. The soldier gripped the handles of a swivel-mounted machine gun, aiming along the side of the train toward the rear cars. More Sarawakan soldiers on foot and armed with assault rifles formed a line in front of the APC, sweat trickling from under their helmets as they scowled at the machine gunner's targets.

The doors near Stone and Caitlyn hissed open. An officer with epaulettes like heaped scrambled eggs on his khaki shoulders boarded, followed by three soldiers. Under the officer's sharp tongue, the soldiers went by Stone and Caitlyn without a glance and took up positions near the rear door of the first-class car. The muzzles of unslung assault rifles covered the window in the rear door and the thick, accordion-pleated rubber gangway to the rest of the train. The officer tested the lock on the rear door, then spoke into a mic clipped inside his sleeve cuff and fell in behind his men.

The train car's thin windows failed to muffle the tramp of hundreds of feet on the dock and the muttering of hundreds of voices in a language Stone couldn't identify. A young child's confused cry burst forth, followed by Sarawakan soldiers brandishing assault rifles and shouting in Malay and English.

The train rocked faintly as the resettled boarded the cars behind Stone and Caitlyn. Distant doors slammed and a clamor of voices went up, audible through the gangway and the first-class car's sealed door.

The officer touched his earbud in an effort to block the tumult, then muttered into his cuff mic. The train lurched into motion. The officer grabbed at an overhead bar and stayed on his feet.

Caitlyn twisted in her seat. Her hand gripped the top of the backrest. Her hazel eyes drooped as she watched the window in the rear door.

The hell? Her pointless question about how the resettled would ride to Trinity came back. *The resettled are going to Trinity. It doesn't matter how.*

She turned her dolorous gaze on him. *Is this our job? Helping third world dictators ethnically cleanse their countries of their opponents?*

Our job is to stop someone on Trinity from finding a lost warpdrive ship.

You know what I mean.

Stone blinked. The dazzling reflection off the nuclear terrorism memorial's onyx curve appeared in his mind's eye. *Better they get exiled than we suffer another Time of Troubles.*

A long silence followed. *Are we?* Caitlyn shifted to face him.

Preventing a repeat of last century's disasters, I mean. Or are we only delaying it?

Delay it long enough and you've prevented it. Stone raised his index finger to waggle it at her. Something in her expression led him to drop it. *Holbrook and Gray can worry about what it all means. We've got our orders. Can I rely on you, or are you going to flake out fretting about things above your pay grade?*

She gave him a look of stung pride. *You can rely on me. Just like you did on Freeland.*

The concrete-block city fell behind. Twenty-foot fences flanked the railroad tracks, with a sandy road just outside, tufted with clumps of grasses between the wheel ruts. Caitlyn had revealed some skill in tradecraft in their prior mission together, along with enough of her limitations for him to know what not to ask of her. Stone showed his palms. *Good to know.*

The train sped past a guard tower, granting a glimpse of a Sarawakan soldier leaning on the railing and vaping. Just outside the fences towered vine-smothered trees. Smooth cuts marked branches pruned back from the sandy road. Cleared for observation and free fire along the fences. Designed to keep locals from illegally crossing the wormhole, or resettleds from choosing a foreign country on Earth over permanent interstellar exile.

Or both.

Stone shrugged to himself. Above his pay grade, too. He leaned back against the scratchy backrest while the train barreled onward.

The train entered the wormhole at full speed. The seat back in front of him and Caitlyn to his side stretched away. Red discolored everything for a moment. Then Stone's weight doubled, pulling his butt and upper legs deeper into the seat. His vision returned to normal, except the morning on Borneo suddenly seemed half as bright.

Frightened cries seeped through the pleated rubber passageway from the cars full of resettled. The shadow of the Earthside equilibrator ring swept across their window.

Everything in Stone's vision suddenly crowded together. He squinted, then squeezed his eyes shut. Sharp blue light seeped through his eyelids. The resettled cried again. Someone shrieked in broken English about going blind.

The blue-tinged lightness rapidly drained. He suddenly felt lighter —his next inhalation seemed to fill his lungs like a balloon, ready to float away. Trinity's surface gravity was 0.84 g. Near the pleated door, the Sarawakan officer muttered to his men in a tone demanding continued alertness. The cries from the car behind lost their terror and quietened a little into a confused gabble.

A twinge of pity came up from the Becker persona. Hundreds of people back there, yanked from their homes, herded onto ships and train cars—

Stone sniffed out a breath. Multiply by a million, and you had the last two centuries of Earth history in a nutshell.

The Becker persona continued its line of thought. —Hundreds of people sent through a hole in space generated by powers beyond their comprehension. God knows what superstitious legends about wormholes and the colonies go whispering through shantytowns and refugee camps on Earth.

It would take a god to care.

The Becker persona slinked away, far below Stone's consciousness.

Caitlyn turned to the window. Still young enough to crave a deep look at each new world. Stone glanced out the windows on the other side. Thin, yellow-orange moonlight—planetlight, technically, if he remembered Gray's briefing—revealed a rolling, rocky plain strewn with stones and boulders.

"Night on Trinity is three weeks long," Caitlyn said. "It's now five days in, sixteen to go."

A dark blur of trees filled the view, broken by stream. As the train crossed the bridge, the gap in the trees revealed spotlights glowing at the eaves of a long, low building with rounded walls.

"A bioseeding facility," she said. "Of the four main bioseeding strategies, Trinity implements...." Caitlyn scowled over her shoulder. "You really don't care how colonists create terrestrial biospheres on their planets?"

"No." Stone added, out of earshot of hidden microphones, *We're here for work. Every planet is Brooklyn.*

Clouds dimmed Bethany's orange-yellow light. The small forest fell behind. Sinuous, parallel lines of tall grains—farmland—came into view on both sides of the train, running from just outside the security fence into the distance.

He glanced at his wristwatch. The platinum hands wound back, presumably syncing with Trinity's local clock. A few minutes after ten. "AM or PM?"

Caitlyn looked at him, then down at his wrist. "PM. Trinity's founders didn't try to correlate their clock with the planet's day-night cycle. The local clock is synced to US Central time."

The train slowed and curved to the left, bringing a new vista into view on the far side of miles of fields. Dim lights shone in the windows of thousands of low buildings. Church steeples and a three-story hospital jutted into the sky. The shantytown of the resettled.

Caitlyn's gaze slid to the shantytown, then darted away, like a tongue probing a missing tooth. Her face hid whatever feelings the shantytown might stir in her.

Keep your head in the game, keyhole kop.

The train plunged through a region of midrise buildings blocking the view of the shantytown. Spotlights shone bright white light on clean walls of concrete block and 3d-printed plastic. More spotlights illuminated UN flags drooping atop poles, and signs identifying by names and logos a dozen UN agencies. Rain fell now; thick drops burst on Caitlyn's window and trickled down the pane.

Stone's gaze roved through the rain among the UN buildings for UNAIM's facility. Location or rainfall made it too difficult to see.

Travelling more slowly with each moment, the train approached the station. Slatted grooves divided a broad concrete platform into dozens of squares ten feet on a side. At the back of the platform, a concrete-block building two stories hide stretched the platform's full width. A gigantic cross of welded steel jutted from the building's upper face, with the words *Welcome to Trinity* underneath in English. To the sides, smaller text repeated the message in twenty other languages. Under the main greeting, more text read *"Now therefore arise, go over this Jordan, thou, and all this people, unto the land which I do give to them."*

Below the lofty words, a series of doors revealed the building's purposes, customs and border control.

Steel half-arches mounted on the building's roof curved above the platform and the track, holding up a translucent roof of thick plastic. The train slowed further. The rattle of rain on the roof reached Stone over the clank of wheels on rails.

A long squeak, and the train stopped. The crowd in the cars behind Stone and Caitlyn shouted and their car rocked with a frantic surge of the resettled.

The Sarawakan officer snapped out a few words in Malay. Safeties on his men's rifles snicked off. The rocking motion ebbed away, but the plaint of anguished voices leaked through from the car behind.

Stone yawned. Every planet is Brooklyn. The door slid back and a conveyor chugged in the luggage compartment below.

Time to go to work.

CHAPTER 6

The UN Travellers Assistance Bureau filled half of the uppermost floor of a four-story building. In the lobby, behind a blue cultured stone counter, wrinkles splayed around a clerk's soft brown eyes. "I'm afraid Mr. Matthews is busy right now," he said with a trace of a South Asian accent. "One of our other advisors could—"

"We'll wait for him," Stone said.

The clerk twisted in his seat. A wall clock read 9:07 AM. "It may be thirty minutes—"

"We'll wait for him."

"You have the right to do so, of course, Mr. Becker. If you would be so kind as to wait in the lobby?"

In his years working for Gray, Stone had waited longer, in far more dangerous locations than this. He touched Caitlyn's elbow. Something in his shoulder twinged—he'd slept on the pull-out couch in their hotel room, and the thin mattress let the steel frame jab him all night. He winced and led her toward the far side of the room.

Picture windows looked out on the straight lines of the UN quarter and the leafy streets of Anderson City beyond. Dominating the city's skyline, a large church—maybe a cathedral, whatever the difference might be—thrust a prism of steel and black glass into the sky. Under gray rainclouds, a white cross at the prism's highest point glowed in the beams of ground-mounted spotlights.

"Look at the size of that thing," Stone muttered. "I hope they haven't fallen into idolatry."

Caitlyn sighed like a wife resigned to her husband's stubbornness. "They love the Lord enough to put up a reminder of His sacrifice."

"I hope you're right."

"What else could it be?"

"A sign they love themselves."

They stood side-by-side in silence for a moment, then Caitlyn went to a cushy red armchair. Her hazel eyes scanned a blank swath of the far wall, a sign she read text projected by her implantable into her optic nerves. Angela usually read passages of scripture while waiting.

Stone turned back to the window. The edge of Trinity's colonized plateau lay somewhere beyond the city, but rain and distance hid the edge from view.

"Mr. and Mrs. Becker?" said the clerk. "Mr. Matthews is ready now."

A green line blazed in Stone's vision. Caitlyn rose and followed him down a hallway. Hidden speakers played a mellow sitar remix of a decades-old pop song from Earth. Framed video loops on the right-hand wall showed Trinity tourist attractions. Most resembled sites on other planets. A decommissioned orbit-to-ground shuttle in a field of resolidified rock. Every colony memorialized the site where its founders first touched boots to ground. Whatever. If Manhattan didn't have a first-landing memorial, no backwater planet needed one either.

One video loop caught Stone's eye. Whitewater roared where a river tumbled off the plateau into a mass of cloud five miles thick.

To their left, windows looked into the offices of travellers assistance advisors. UN employees of different races, sons and daughters of the ruling classes that had filled the previous day's train with resettled. The UN employees stared at whatever their devices projected onto blank spots on their walls. Working hard. Yeah, right.

The final office on the left also had windows, but here, lowered blinds turned closed vertical slats to the hallway. A sliver of LED light emerged from the slightly open door. Stone knocked, inches from the door's *V. Matthews* nameplate.

"Come in." Matthews' voice barely overcame the hallway's mellow sitar music.

Stone pushed open the door and followed Caitlyn inside. He rested his hand on the inside door handle and surveyed the room. A glass-door cabinet, eight feet high, three wide, and two deep, stood against the wall to the right of Matthews' cramped desk. The cabinet displayed bibles faced in leather or quilted fabric—local handicrafts, probably.

The massive cabinet dominated the room and made Matthews behind his desk look like a lonely child. White LEDs heightened the pallor of his sunken cheeks. "Welcome to Trinity. How may I help you?"

A push on the door handle and the door thumped shut. Matthews' eyebrows jumped. For a moment, silence reigned.

Stone leaned forward. "'It's not enough to nuke the site from orbit.'"

"'You need boots on the ground to make sure,'" Caitlyn said.

Abruptly, Matthews looked through them, presumably at privately-projected data. The door's bolt locked with a snick. He turned to his right, away from the whisper of rubber wheels coming from the display cabinet. Some conditioning or post-hypnotic suggestion. Torture or truth serum wouldn't extract this room's secrets from him.

The gap between the cabinet and the wall enlarged. The wall bore a hole, about six and a half feet high and two wide. The hole gave access to a vertical shaft, two feet deep with a ladder on the far side.

You should go first, Caitlyn said.

I know. Stone slipped behind the counter, reached for the ladder. A musty smell wrinkled his nose. Battery-powered puck lights glowed on the walls and smeared reflections on the ladder's steel rungs. Caitlyn's footsteps sounded just above his descending hands. Her perfume drifted to his nose. Floral but lacking any pheromones. Subtle.

His feet touched rough concrete as a motor above them hummed. The rubber wheels of the cabinet rolled again. The pallid light from Matthews' office narrowed, then vanished.

The puck lights gave enough illumination to reveal a handle and the seam of a low, closed door in the wall to the left of the ladder. Stone sidled over and Caitlyn shuffled next to him. Their breaths sounded loud in the cramped space. Stone turned the handle and pushed. Hard. The door nudged open. He pushed harder, widening the gap enough. They hunched over and went through…

…into an office crowded with unused desks and bookcases. A man sat on the corner of a bare desk, catching his breath. His beige plaid suit jacket gapped away from the back of his shirt collar. From under thick black eyebrows and a high, craggy brow, he impassively watched Stone enter, but his eyes widened slightly when Caitlyn stood up and shook out her long blond hair.

His brows lowered. Stone read his expression as a request to shut the door behind him. He reached back, found an empty bookcase affixed to the door. A little pressure on the bookcase and the entire assembly easily swung shut.

The man's brows remained low. "I'm Georgeakis. I run the field office."

"Codename Hybrid." Retina scanners and body aroma analyzers hidden somewhere in the room would confirm Stone's identity, if they hadn't already.

"All the way from headquarters, huh?" Georgeakis swung his left leg over the corner of the desk and he dropped his feet to the floor. Four inches shorter than Stone, not counting the chip on his shoulder. "You think being one of Gray's finest gives you the right to sneak a woman in?"

Caitlyn sniffed out a breath.

"She's working with me," Stone said.

Georgeakis folded his arms. "Gray never sends two operatives."

"He only sent one. Blondie works for another agency. She and I are collaborating on this mission."

Blondie? she enunciated.

I don't know your codename. I wouldn't share it if I did.

Georgeakis breathed through gritted teeth for a moment. Then his shoulders slumped and he spoke with resignation. "You're investigating the illegal entry and murder at the UNAIM facility the other night."

"Exactly. So tell me what you know."

"Didn't you read my reports?" Georgeakis asked with an edgy voice.

"No," Stone said nonchalantly. "They give me preconceptions I'd have to dispel after I talk to the field office."

Caitlyn laughed. "In other words, he's too lazy—"

"Lady," Georgeakis said, but he sounded unconvinced she really was one, "I guessed that already."

After a moment, Caitlyn said, "I for one did read your reports."

"Great. Why don't you brief him and I'll just fill in the gaps."

Caitlyn nodded. "I'd be glad to. By the way, I appreciate your hard work. Without strong efforts by field offices, we'd be flying blind."

Georgeakis grunted, but the corners of his mouth lifted in a smile that touched the sides of his eyes. Stone bit back a subvocal rejoinder to her. A little flattery could go far. *Okay, you play good cop.*

I already have. "About forty-eight hours ago, the body of a resettled male was found eighty yards outside the shantytown fence. Shirtless, patched trousers, three GSWs to the chest. No identification, but his DNA profile matched a security guard, Thomas Chanongo, recently hired by UNAIM. The UN constabulary began investigating over the protests of the Trinity police."

"Go on," Stone said.

"The constabulary tracked Chanongo's last known location to the UNAIM facility. They found evidence of a break-in at the facility— resoldered alarm wires and rewelded cuts in the perimeter fencing. They also found traces of Chanongo's blood inside a computer work- room. The blood smear pattern fit with Chanongo getting shot in that workroom, and his killer cleaning his blood almost thoroughly enough to avoid detection."

Stone thought aloud. "The killer wasn't an amateur. And he wanted no one to know he infiltrated the UNAIM facility. What else do we know?"

Caitlyn turned her hazel eyes on Georgeakis. "The latest report I've seen from you came in yesterday morning Trinity time. Twenty-four hours ago. Anything new?"

"Yes, of course, I just haven't written it up yet. The constabulary is smart enough to realize that any fab plans that might have been stolen from UNAIM are only useful if the thieves have a fabricator. They didn't fab anything at UNAIM on the night of the murder. All fabs used by UN agencies, or loaned by the UN to locals, have backdoors that the constabulary can use to check system logs for the past week. Those are all clean. No unauthorized use."

Stone peered at Georgeakis. "Has the constabulary checked the Trinity colonists' fabs?"

"They're working on it. It's a bigger challenge than looking for unauthorized use. They gotta sift normal usage patterns for anomalous activity. They say it could take days." Georgeakis raised his palms. "I know, they're just constabulary, they gotta hire people Gray'd turn away. But I think they're telling the truth. A hundred civilian fabs generate a crap-ton of usage data every day."

"We'd like copies of that usage data," Caitlyn said.

What? Stone asked. ITB trains its operatives in data mining?

A little. But more importantly, you and I know what to look for, which the constabulary doesn't. Besides, would you rather do something, or pace around the hotel room waiting for a call? To Georgeakis, she said, "Can you pull the civilian fab usage data?"

Georgeakis stiffened his back. "Easily," he said in a voice tinged with stung pride. "Fifteen minutes, tops, to copy it from the constabulary's server."

Her eyes widened. "That quickly? Hybrid here isn't the only one of Gray's finest."

"Just doing my job. And ask Gray if he's hiring. My guys would love to work with field operatives like you."

She angled her head a fraction down, to let her blond hair partially cover her cheeks. "Thank you, Mr. Georgeakis."

The head of the field office left the room. Stone and Caitlyn waited in the cramped space until he came back. 14:14 later, according to Stone's implantable. "Here you go," Georgeakis said.

A window popped up in Stone's vision. Terabytes of data, scanned for viruses, UNICA's chain of custody verified and validated with Georgeakis' visual signature. Stone focused on the *OK* button and blinked.

Ten seconds later, the progress bar reached 100% and blinked out of his vision.

"Time to go, Blondie." He went between Caitlyn and Georgeakis and tugged on the side panel of the bookcase. It swung open, revealing the low doorway into the shaft. Stone held the bookcase until Caitlyn went through.

The display case's motor hummed when Caitlyn took her first step on the ladder. Matthews might not have moved the entire time they'd been below—his narrow back and hunched shoulders faced the opening until the display case rolled back against the wall. Then he turned to Stone and Caitlyn. After his blank expression induced by the code phrase, the faint warmth in his face made him seem as exuberant as a rockstar. "Enjoy the rest of your stay on Trinity."

Stone put on a smirk. "I'm sure we will."

CHAPTER 7

Five hours later, terabytes of alphanumeric gobbledygook scrolled up the inside of Stone's lids whenever he shut his eyes. He lolled his head back against the hotel suite's sofa and squeezed his eyes further shut. No help. The data logs from Trinity's fabs outside direct UN control kept taunting him with afterimages. "Your plan failed," he muttered.

"It only means the thieves haven't started fabbing anything using stolen plans." Caitlyn's voice dripped defensiveness.

Stone lifted his head, opened his eyes. "Do you have another idea?"

The corners of her hazel eyes crinkled. She took a deep, sudden interest in the weave of the suite's carpet. "Off hand, all I can think of is we recon each fab location. Or wait until the thieves start fabbing spaceship parts."

Stone climbed off the couch and paced across the hotel suite's living area. He yanked back the blackout and sheer curtains. The streets glistened. Bethany bled yellow-orange light through gashes in the clouds. Superimposed on the cathedral's black prism were his reflection and Caitlyn's. Her interest in the carpet weave shifted to the other side of the room.

"We must be missing something." He returned his attention to the night-dark view outside. The small, low-rise downtown of a small city on a backwater planet. A total of 107 fabs. Even if they were all located in Anderson City, casing each one would take hours. If some were scattered over the colonized plateau, the time frame would climb to days.

If they waited until the thieves used a fab for spaceship parts, they might wait forever.

He lifted his head, sniffing an idea as if it were a trace of perfume. Set aside *when*. *Where*. "I'm going to look at something."

"What?"

He returned to the sofa. The cloth-covered cushions behind his back were far more comfortable than the fold-out mattress.

"What are you looking at?" Caitlyn asked with an exasperated edge.

He didn't answer.

She soon sniffed out a breath. "You and your alpha game crap."

Idly, Stone waved off her chatter. He reopened fab logs and skimmed them one by one. He ignored the thousands of timestamped lines in the body of each log. Instead, he focused on the header blocks, listing each fab's owner, location, and service information.

Of the fabs on Trinity outside direct UN control, 91 belonged to Trinity Global Products, the public utility providing necessities—foodstuffs, clothing, medicine, and household goods—not yielded by the farmland outside the city. Stone told his implantable to pop locations on a map. Except for the few in outlying small towns, TGP's fabs clustered by fives and sixes at facilities around Anderson City.

Stone subvoked to his implantable. It projected into his vision a slideshow of videos of TGP facilities. Industrial park buildings, where trucks blazoned with the TGP logo constantly backed up to the loading docks. Three shifts of people directed robotic arms to sling fabbed products into the backs of the trucks. True both in the city and the outlying small towns.

With that many people around, someone would notice the loading of sheets of hull alloys or the long, slender parabolas of fusion drive nozzles. Especially into a truck that didn't belong to TGP.

Skip those 91, for now. Sixteen fabs yet to review.

Seven belonged to agencies of the colonists' government. The bioseeding department owned five, operating one at each of five locations like the one glimpsed from the train the night before. Probably dedicated to greenhouse and hydroponic parts, genetech equipment, off-road vehicles, tools, fertilizer. Isolated locations, with plenty of off-duty time.

Stone moved the five bioseeding fabs to the short list.

One of the two remaining Trinity government fabs belonged to the planet-wide police department. Probably for production of body armor, handguns, and ammunition. Possibly also mind-altering drugs and CRISPR brain vectors for prisoner rehabilitation.

Stone recalled the vast sprawling shantytown huddled under the clouding nighttime sky, and Gray's comment that resettled outnumbered colonists sixteen-to-one. Add armored personnel carriers, water cannons, autonomous drones, and sniper rifles to the list.

Certainly a chance the Trinity police could use their fab to build spaceship parts. They'd tried to keep the UN constabulary from investigating the security guard's murder, which would make sense if they'd been involved. Police knew how burglars broke in and entered buildings and could use the same techniques. Their fab would have limited access—yes. The header block gave its location as a facility forty miles from Anderson City, on the edge of the plateau. A steep, five mile slope smothered with clouds on one side, and a quarter-million acres of tropical rain forest on the other.

The Trinity police fab had been offline for maintenance for three days.

The last government fab belonged to the Church of Trinity. Stone's eyebrow rose, then he shrugged. Every government had a state religion. Trinity's worshipped a god instead of abstract rhetoric about *freedom* and *democracy*.

He blinked away the idle thoughts. The Church of Trinity housed its fab in downtown Anderson City, in a maintenance building in the unmoving shadow of the cathedral's black prism.

What the hell would a church need to fab? Bibles and hymnals on printed paper? Stained glass windows? Wafers and wine for Communion?

The Tobias Becker persona nudged his awareness. *As ye have done it unto one of the least of these my brethren, ye have done it unto me.* The Church might fab non-perishable food and serviceable clothing for charity.

The sprawling shantytown could consume every molecule of charity the Church might fabricate.

Still, the Church's fab could have uncommitted time. An interplanetary ship's drive nozzle could fit on a medium-sized truck and ride unremarked through downtown Anderson City at two a.m. He filed the Church's fab as a possibility.

Nine remaining fabs. In civilian hands, but doubtless heavily regulated by the colonists' government. Two belonged to companies that fabbed agricultural chemicals, mostly fertilizers and insect pheromones to entice pollinators. One fabbed seeds of genetech crop plants. One built luxury products for consumers with enough money to avoid rationing and the stigma of sharing TGP's output with the masses. The other four fabs belonged to a manufacturer of factory equipment and heavy machinery.

Stone checked the locations of the heavy equipment company's four fabs. A warm thrill ran up his arms and legs.

One of its fabs, offline for four days, had recently been relocated. It now was sited forty miles from Anderson City, on the edge of the plateau. Next to a steep slope hidden under dense cloud cover.

"Found them." He strode to the minibar.

Caitlyn's brows crinkled. "Found what?"

"The two fabs that are going to produce the spaceship parts." He cracked open a bottle of sparkling water, poured. He turned to her and sipped through a grin.

"Like hell."

His grin turned to a smirk. "Don't blame me that your idea failed. I'll beam you my findings." He subvoked to his implantable. It popped a green thumbs-up icon onto his vision after it transmitted the message.

She sat still for a minute while her hazel eyes darted. Her mouth opened and she looked up. "You might be right."

"*Might?*"

"It's a possibility. But what do we do with it?"

"Find a way inside that facility. As soon as possible."

"We need time to plan." She idly shook her head. "Or do you want to just drive up to the front gate?"

"Hmm. Good idea. Bold and unexpected."

She scowled at him. "Don't get sarcastic with me."

A grin split his face. "When do I ever get sarcastic with anyone?"

CHAPTER 8

Their headlights showed a narrow, rocky track between dark green trees entwined by creeping vines. The rental coupe crept along, but the uneven pathway repeatedly jostled the car and punched Stone and Caitlyn's backsides through the bucket seats facing forward from the rear of the coupe's cabin. Bethany remained in its spot slightly north of zenith and sent narrow bands of light almost straight down the insides of the windows.

"The facility formerly belonged to Trinity's bioseeding department," Caitlyn said. "Bioseeding decommissioned it after this rainforest reached maturity."

Stone yawned. Mid-afternoon both in local time and back in Manhattan. The extra speedlearning on the suborbital flight, combined with Bethany overhead like a gigantic three-quarter moon, must have disrupted his body clock more than usual. He squeezed shut his eyes and shook his head. "How far away?"

"Two miles."

His implantable popped an ETA into a corner of his vision: 5:58, 5:57, 5:56.... "They've made us by now. They have automated surveillance this far from their facility."

She twisted in her seat. Too dark to see her hazel eyes, yet by the way she held her head she plainly doubted him. "How can you tell?"

"How long have I been doing this?"

Caitlyn shifted away from him.

Stone went on. "The only question is how far out they'll set guards."

"This far out will make it obvious they're hiding something."

"Exactly."

The adaptive headlights blazed the trail as the car rounded a corner, jumped when a wheel hit a pothole. Mottled gray track littered with gravel-sized fragments of the same rock. Overhanging limbs with cauterized stumps. Trinity PD clearly spent time maintaining the track against the ever-growing jungle. No guards, though. The same after another curve. Seconds crept by. 1:41, 1:40, 1:39—

"Half a mile," Caitlyn said. The rental started up a slope, where gravel lay in ruts left by truck tires and heavy rains. Traction control pulsed the brakes of slipping wheels.

At the top of the slope, the rental stopped abruptly. The headlights lit up a closed gate of steel piping, flanked by a tall wire fence running away from the sides of the road into the rain forest. In front of the gate stood a pair of guards in blue police uniforms. Snap flaps covered their holstered sidearms. One came forward, leading with a sachet of dipping tobacco bulging between his cheek and lower jaw.

"Ready?" Stone asked.

"Absolutely. You can count on me."

"I assumed I could, but is there a reason I shouldn't?"

Caitlyn stiffened her back and pressed together her full lips.

Outside, the lead guard caught Stone's gaze. The guard gestured like he reeled in a fish.

"Open the window," Stone told the rental. He rested his hands on his thighs. Glanced at Caitlyn. She did the same as the electric motor whirred. Warm, humid air and a whiff of rotting leaves drifted into the cabin. "God be with you, officer."

"And also with you." A pungent tobacco scent drifted in on his breath. "You folks are from Earth?"

"That's right. How could—do I have an accent?"

"Enough of one. Now, I don't mean to be rude to tourists—we'd love more of you and a lot less of the kind of folks the UN shoves through the wormhole—but this area is restricted. Time to back down-hill, turn around, and head back to the city. Plenty of other places to hike in the rain for—"

"No," Stone said. "We're here because this area is restricted."

The second guard backed away. A snap sounded at his belt despite the slow motion of his hand at his holster flap.

The lead guard worked his tobacco sachet to the other side of his mouth with a slow, lip-distending movement of his tongue. "You'd best drive away now, sir."

Stone slowly raised his palms. "Tell your bosses that we know what they're going to fab. The UN secret police know it too. If your bosses let us in, we can help them get away with it."

The lead guard glanced past Stone. "Ma'am, you've been very quiet. You have anything to say?"

"Do you know what your superiors are going to fab?"

The lead guard drew out his reply. "No."

"Then I have nothing to say. For your own protection."

A sniffed-out breath answered her.

Stone spoke. "Before you call your bosses, you can put their mind at ease. I have something on the floor near my feet. May I pick it up?"

The lead guard came closer and angled his head. His gaze landed on a paper lunch sack, partially mangled. "Go ahead."

Slowly, Stone picked up the sack. Plastic and metal rattled inside. "I pulled the rental company's tracking widget from inside the wheel well and stomped on it. All the parts should be in here."

"While he did that," Caitlyn added, "I turned off the car's web access. It can't report its location to the rental company. Or anyone else."

Stone put on a chummy smile. "Go ahead and call. We'll wait. Roll up the window."

The rental followed his order as the guard backed away. In the headlights' glow, the two guards conferred. Puzzled expressions, agitated arm motions. The tobacco sachet squirmed inside the lead guard's closed mouth.

Five minutes later, the other guard nodded. He slipped into a narrow guardhouse, smaller than a public toilet stall in Central Park. The lead guard watched Caitlyn and Stone, his hands on his belt, elbows wide, tobacco sachet at the lower front of his mouth like a shield.

Would Stone remember the tobacco sachet if he had to kill the man? The littlest details sometimes clung to his memory, swirling together into a mosaic of patchy memories.

Stone shook his head to derail his train of thought.

Fifteen minutes crept by. Enough time for wispy clouds to extend tendrils toward the car from the edge of the plateau, a half-mile ahead and hidden by dense foliage.

Twin cones of light bobbed toward them, where the track continued on the other side of the gate. A hummvee, painted a flat and dusty shade of white, riding on broad, knobby tires. The vehicle stopped on the far side of the gate. The double doors on the left side swung apart.

A man emerged. Tall and lean, his sunken eyes gazed between the gate's crossbars and over the rental car. Bethany's yellow-orange light gleamed on his bald scalp. If he lived on Earth, Stone would have guessed his age between forty and ninety; on a colony, the tall man would be no more than sixty.

He dressed like a police detective or FBI agent from a costume drama: charcoal-gray suit and a thickly-knotted red necktie. Despite the suit and his black leather monkstrap shoes, he scaled the gate like a long-legged spider and dropped deftly to the ground near the guardhouse.

He peered at Stone and mouthed something, followed by a sharp get-out gesture. He raised his voice enough to reach the rental's cabin. "Come with me!"

"Open up," Stone told the rental.

The doors popped open, swung wide. Stone climbed out, then reached back for Caitlyn's hand. She slid across the seat. Knees of her capri pants pressed together, she swung her lower legs to the ground. Stone pulled her up. Only then did he turn to the bald man with sunken eyes. "How do you do, Agent—?"

"Intros later. Tell your car to turn around and go 3.6 miles. There, we need it to turn left at an unmarked dirt road. We'll guide it by transponder from there to a garage."

"Whatever you say," Stone said.

Caitlyn rested her slender fingers on the rental's roof. Bent her head to speak into the cabin. She stepped back and the rental shut its doors. Seconds later it showed its taillights as it descended the slope.

"Open the gate," the tall, bald man told the guards.

Tobacco sachet bulging his upper lip, the lead guard nodded, went into the guardhouse, tapped buttons. The gate swung inward with a hum of electric motors.

"Frisk them."

The second guard said, "Right away." He reached into the guardhouse and emerged holding an eighteen-inch gray plastic rod with clear beads projecting from the tip.

"Did I say scan them?" His sunken eyes were like the open doors of solitary confinement cells.

"We're sharing the load, sir," the lead guard said. He rested a knee on the rocky ground and patted down Stone's ankle and lower leg. The second guard swept the rod's tip up and down Caitlyn's body from six inches away.

Stone and Caitlyn's pistols rested in their hotel suite's locked safe. All according to plan.

The guards backed away and nodded. The bald man jerked his thumb over his shoulder. "Ride with me," he said to Stone and Caitlyn.

Vat-grown leather covering the rear seats creaked as they sat. Bulbs recessed in the ceiling poured pallid light over them. The bald man sat in the front seats, facing them across the cabin. The doors thumped shut. Air conditioning whined to battle the remaining traces of humid, pungent air.

The hummvee executed a three-point turn. No control panels or overrides visible. It started down the track toward the plateau's edge. The green masses of leaves and vines on each side crept by. The tall, bald man said, "I'm Special Agent Laclede. Your names?"

"Tobias Becker."

"Angela."

Laclede stretched his long arm across the backrest. "You have a minute to tell me what you think you know and how you came to know it."

Stone leaned forward. Knees apart, he rested his forearms on his thighs, palms up. "Someone broke into the UNAIM facility and killed a security guard, three nights ago. The perpetrators could have stolen fab code for advanced equipment UNAIM doesn't share with colonials. Around that time, two Trinity colonial fabs went offline. Those two fabs are still offline, but both of them report their location as that facility I can glimpse through the trees behind you."

Laclede's thin eyebrows flexed up. Three millimeters, half a second. More than enough.

Stone went on. "We came to help you fab that advanced equipment without the UN secret police finding out."

"That's it?" Laclede bent his long arm and extended his index finger. Forearm and finger aimed at Stone's heart. "You've told me what you think you know—"

"And I'll tell you how we found it," Caitlyn said. Her hazel eyes flashed. "We're UN secret police sent from Earth to investigate the break-in."

Laclede bent his long arm further, moving his hand toward the pistol fairly well hidden inside his suit jacket. "Are you now?"

Caitlyn lifted and spread her fingers. Her trimmed nails gleamed in the spotlights. "The UN doesn't know that God has called on us to betray it."

CHAPTER 9

The last of the rainforest fell away, revealing the former bioseeding facility. Swooping concrete lines dappled with three stories of windows marked the main building. An array of six long, low greenhouses lay between the main building and the rainforest's edge. Dust grimed the greenhouses' walls and overgrown vegetation squeezed under peaked roofs. In the distance, a mass of gray tinged with orange and yellow gyrated—the top of the cloudbank smothering the lowlands.

The hummvee followed the track between greenhouses, then descended a ramp toward a vehicle entrance. Inside, it rolled through a space of concrete stark under bright white LED banks. The Trinity PD logo showed on the sides of open-topped armored cars painted in urban camouflage and man-sized drones with sky-blue under-carriages.

A turn. A pulse of brakes. The hummvee stopped near a gray metallic elevator door in a vast concrete wall. Three uniformed policemen stood in a line to the vehicle's left. The doors on that side of hummvee popped open.

Laclede flicked the backs of his fingers toward the open doors. "You two first."

Stone followed Caitlyn out of the hummvee. The policemen turned flat eyes on them. Laclede emerged with a scrape of hard leather soles on the concrete.

The elevator doors pinged open. "Up we go," Laclede said. The uniformed policemen crowded into the elevator car with Stone, Caitlyn, and Laclede. Crowded Stone's nose with cheap cologne and nervous sweat. He could probably take out two of them in these close quarters. Caitlyn might handle one. Scratch that—if it came to a fight, he would have to strike Laclede first. Despite the suit and the dress shoes, Stone sensed Laclede would be more dangerous than all three uniforms put together.

Stone audibly exhaled through his nose. If it came to a fight, he and Caitlyn would have failed.

The elevator car stopped at the top level. The doors rattled open. One of the uniforms led the way down a curving hallway of concrete and exposed steel girders.

He showed Stone and Caitlyn into a high-ceilinged lounge full of overstuffed armchairs. A wet bar stood to the left, past twenty feet of swirled concrete floor. Synthetic wood paneled three walls in alternating vertical stripes the colors of copper and honey. The paneling's grains and textures looked almost real. The fourth wall consisted of picture windows, separated by exposed girders, looking out on the cloud mass obscuring the lowlands.

In front of the middle picture window, with his back to the door, stood a man. His hands were clasped behind his tailored indigo suit. Short but disheveled brown hair, interspersed with single strands of white, crowned his head.

Laclede cleared his throat.

The man in the indigo suit turned. Half a head shorter than Laclede, wearing wire-framed eyeglasses he doubtless used as a display device, his brown eyes blazed from below his high forehead as if they were magnets. All the policemen, Laclede included, oriented to him like iron filings.

To Stone and Caitlyn, the man said, "I'm Paul Ulrich, CEO of Ulrich Industrial Equipment. How do you do, Mr. and Mrs. Becker." His voice was quiet but still carried through the room. Ulrich strode toward Caitlyn and Stone, in turn shook their hands. His smooth grip matched Stone's for firmness; he swept his free hand over the back of Caitlyn's. "Let us sit."

Caitlyn and Stone took a high-backed crimson loveseat. Their thighs brushed together and she shifted her legs a couple of inches away from him—

No, he subvoked privately to her. *Keep up the act.*

No reply, but her weight shifted and her leg pressed warmly against his.

Ulrich sat in an armchair of the same color that half faced the loveseat. After a glance from Ulrich, Laclede settled his long frame into a deep yellow-tan armchair to Ulrich's right and opposite Stone and Caitlyn. The uniformed policeman lined up along the wall containing the door to the hallway.

Stone leaned forward. Ulrich seemed the type to get down to business.

Instead, Ulrich said, "Let us pray."

Pray? Stone subvoked to Caitlyn.

When in Rome.

Ulrich shut his eyes and nested his palms face-up in his lap. Stone did the same. A moment later, Ulrich spoke. "Heavenly Father, we here, Your servants, humbly ask for Your guidance in doing what is right for Your people, both on Trinity and on Earth, now and forevermore...."

How could someone who commanded the respect of Laclede and the other policemen with such authority say such treacly things?

"...We ask in the name of Your Son, Jesus, the Christ, Who taught us to pray, saying—"

The Tobias Becker pushed the words out of Stone's mouth in unison with Ulrich's. "'Our Father, Who art in Heaven....'" He continued speaking the rote text, whatever it was—the Lord's Prayer, according to Tobias Becker. Caitlyn's mellow voice flowed the same words into his left ear. Stone and Caitlyn's voices spewed sibilants in 'trespasses,' but the Becker personas recovered quickly and matched the locals in the next line. '...as we forgive our debtors....'"

The Lord's Prayer soon ended. "Amen," Laclede said quickly, as if slightly embarrassed by Ulrich's piety. Stone and Caitlyn each echoed the word.

Ulrich opened his eyes. Intense brown irises aimed at Caitlyn and Stone like handgun muzzles. "I believe you two are UN secret agents. I'm unconvinced you are Christians."

Caitlyn's voice sounded plaintive in Stone's mind's ear. *He's on to us—*

Stick to the plan. Stone spread his hands. "Has the Church of Trinity decreed that reciting *trespasses* in the Lord's Prayer is heretical?"

Ulrich pressed his lips together, his mouth looking for a moment like a frog's. "Don't act coy, Mr. Becker. If that's even your name."

"It's what I was born with."

Ulrich rested his hands on his chair's arms. "My grandfather grew up in the United States in the middle of the last century, when the Whore of Babylon ruled the fallen world from her palace on the Potomac." Ulrich's gaze drilled through Stone, the loveseat cushions, and the synthwood paneling on the wall. "A hundred thousand analysts and agents spied for the United States. My grandfather considered it a given that the number of her spies who were brothers or sisters in Christ could be counted on one hand. Do you disagree?"

Caitlyn leaned forward amid a rustle of blond hair. "That was decades before we were born."

"But you must know the evils her agents inflicted on our brothers and sisters around the world. She aided governments across Africa and Asia in the oppression of Christians. How many millions of believers died in those lands during the Time of Troubles?"

When in doubt, tell the truth. "From what I've read on the worldweb," Stone said, "a few tens of thousands who took up arms in open rebellion against their governments...."

"Dear lord," Caitlyn said, breath tight. "The worldweb lied to us."

Stone turned to her, gripped her hand. "More than that, Angela. Our churches lied to us."

"Our churches? How can that be?"

Ulrich's quiet voice cut through the room. "Because the pastors and leaders of some churches claim to worship our Lord when they secretly serve the king and queen of the fallen world. Back to my point.

What Christian could spy for the Whore of Babylon with a clean conscience?"

Stone shook his head. "You're talking about the United States seventy-five years ago. It's a broken superpower now. We don't work for it. We work for the UN."

"It's a broken superpower because the Whore of Babylon moved her palace to Manhattan and crowned herself queen of the world. Don't fool yourselves. You work for her." Ulrich's gaze harpooned them. "She still oppresses our brothers and sisters and you fully know it. How many Christians did she pack into cattle cars at the back of your train yesterday?"

Caitlyn dropped her gaze. Blond locks slid toward her eyes. "We don't know."

"But you can guess. Hundreds? Perhaps over a thousand? Yesterday. On the same train you traveled here on. Forced onto that train by policies that you two enable." Ulrich's gaze filleted back and forth between Caitlyn and Stone. "So tell me how two Christians can serve with clean consciences as UN secret agents?"

Stone drew in a long breath. Patted Caitlyn's hand. "We can't. Our consciences are so dirty from the choice we made that I—I—" His eyes moistened. He pushed his next words through a tight throat. "Sometimes I doubt that the Lamb has enough blood to wash away all my sins." He squeezed shut his eyes and ducked his head from Ulrich's piercing gaze.

Caitlyn's warm, soft palm smoothed the back of his hand. "All our sins."

He regarded her around droplets of tears clinging to his eyelashes. "No, my love. I chose our path and you followed me. The sin is ultimately mine."

"The Lord will forgive us both. That's why we came to—"

"Enough," commanded Ulrich's quiet voice. "Only the Lord can know your sins and whether your repentance is true. Tell me about the choice you made, Mr. Becker."

Stone sniffled in a breath. "Alright. You should know everything. It goes back to our last months at our university. Angela was finishing her B.S. in physics while I wrote my dissertation for my Master of

Divinity. We'd discussed our dreams of mission work beyond Earth, with ourselves, our pastor, and with friends on social media." He glanced at Caitlyn.

"I'd always assumed the UN secret police gleaned our hopes from our social media posts," she said. She turned her hazel eyes to Ulrich. "But what you just said… maybe our pastor…." She shook her head in disbelief.

"UN recruiters flew from New York to meet us," Stone said. "They almost fooled me into thinking they too served the Lord. 'We want you to spread the Gospel to the colonies in the asteroid belt and the outer solar system. We'll provide a ship and funds to maintain it. Train you to fly it.'"

Laclede's thin eyebrows flashed upward. Ulrich raised his index finger an inch from his chair's arm.

Despite what he'd glimpsed, Stone kept speaking. "'All we ask in return is that you tell us what you see and hear on your journeys,' they told us. 'And if the Gospel takes root in a colony, remind the new believers to *render unto Caesar.*'"

"How many late nights we spent in the tiny living room of my apartment," Caitlyn said, "talking and praying while the sound of the highway came in through the window screens. The UN wanted us to pacify the solar system colonies." Tenderly, to Stone, she said, "You almost convinced me to refuse."

"I almost convinced myself," he said. "But then the Lord told me, deep down, at the place inside where you don't know where your thoughts end and His begin. He told me something very important." His gaze met Ulrich's. "Empires rise and fall. The Church will outlast every one of them."

A close-lipped smile dimpled Ulrich's cheeks. "'I am Alpha and Omega, the beginning and the end.'"

"So we took their offer. No illusions. Open eyes." Stone blew out a breath. "As open as they can be when you're under twenty-five."

Caitlyn patted his hand. "We led hundreds of people to the Lord."

"And passed intel that sent thousands to the grave. The UN officials used us, Mr. Ulrich, far more than we used them."

"They used my father in the same way," Ulrich said, "and he

persuaded a majority of Trinity's leaders to accede to the Dubai Convention. May God have mercy on his soul."

"The UN officials used our intel to implement policies that blew up in our faces," Stone said. "We ended up in an asteroid colony riot that almost cost us our lives...." He looked at Caitlyn with his lips pressed together. Tobias and Angela Becker wouldn't talk about the miscarriage.

"We survived," she said.

He turned to Ulrich. "And after we escaped the asteroid colony, our paymasters demanded their ship back and froze the funds we needed to operate it. Then they ordered us to train for interstellar operations and told us we would never do mission work again. Did your father ever despair after he realized how they'd used him?"

Ulrich straightened his back. "No."

"I did. So many times. Only by remembering the hundreds of people around the solar system we'd brought to Christ did I keep hope alive. But then one late night Angela came home from exotic matter physics training and my hope took wings. Tell him, honey."

"Me?"

"You heard the story first. Tell him."

"Okay, dear." Caitlyn lifted her face to Ulrich. "What do you know about the warpdrive ships that brought your grandfather's generation to Trinity? And what happened to them afterward?"

"We've never gotten the full story from UN officials here," Ulrich said, "but our understanding is the UN seized control of the exotic matter factory, then built a combat fleet that hunted down all the independent pilots like the one who brought us here. Accurate?"

"Mostly," Caitlyn said. "We heard the same story, growing up on Earth, even when spying for the UN under the cover of mission work. I only came to doubt it that night Tobias mentioned. One senior agent, assigned to training duties, was nipping from a flask as the physicist's lecture ended. It loosened his tongue enough to let the truth slip. One warpdrive ship had avoided discovery."

Ulrich's quiet voice challenged her. "How could one ship escape the notice of all the UN's resources?"

"Space is vaster than our planet-born intuitions tell us," Caitlyn said. "The senior agent had some guesses, based on how UN ships operate. They look for gravitational distortions caused by a warpdrive in action. They also scan for metallic objects orbiting the suns, planets, or moons of colony systems. If a ship shut down its warpdrive and were camouflaged with rocky or icy material, the scanners wouldn't find it."

Ulrich's intense brown eyes darted, as if different parts of him grabbed the controls. "They also wouldn't find a ship if it were destroyed in flight. When I was a child, my grandfather told me the founders hired a different ship, *Swan of Cygnus*, to transport the colonists to Trinity after it returned from another run. That ship never returned to Earth. My grandfather and the others assumed it had been destroyed and they hired *Lady Lux* out of desperation."

Stone inhaled, sharply enough that Laclede and Ulrich glanced his way. Holbrook and Gray's records didn't name the missing ship, but let these colonists think *Lady Lux* might be it.

"UN ships scan for deep-space wreckage on every voyage to and from Earth," Caitlyn said. "They've found four destroyed ships. Including *Swan of Cygnus*, outbound with at least eight hundred dead." She shrugged and rolled her wrists. "You're right, the missing ship could have been destroyed and not yet discovered, but the UN believes it's thoroughly scanned every direct route from Earth to any known colony world."

"I see. But the pilot of this missing ship. What would he have done for the past fifty years?"

"We're moving beyond second-hand information to our own speculations, now," Caitlyn said.

"Speculate."

She said, "Coldsleep is a possibility—"

"—not really," Stone said, his tone sounding as if they'd debated this a hundred times. "I never heard of warpdrive ships using coldsleep."

"But the technology existed during the Time of Troubles. Back in Sol System, we met outer system old-timers who'd used it for low energy travel. You must remember."

"I do, but…." Stone waved his hand like an exasperated husband.

"It's a possibility, yes. But with a nanofabricator, a pilot could stay alive and awake for decades."

"For decades? Alone in a living space smaller than this room, eating flavored protein glop recycled from his own feces? A pilot would go stir crazy."

"Any more crazy than those outer system old-timers we met? You must remember." Stone smirked as he spoke the last words.

"He or she would also need hydrogen to power a ship's fusion reactor to keep the nanofabricator running." Caitlyn shook out her hair as if she'd won the point.

Stone chuckled. "He could siphon some water ice camouflaging his ship."

Caitlyn drew in a breath to speak, but Ulrich's quiet tone cut in. "Why would a pilot hide for decades?"

Warmth flashed in her hazel eyes. "Precisely my next point." She drew in a breath, huffed it out. "A third possibility is he's not hiding. He's dead."

"More likely than coldsleep." Stone nodded. "Accidents happen."

"And isolated souls...." Caitlyn shrank in on herself. "May destroy themselves out of loneliness and despair."

Stone lowered his gaze. "They may."

"Enough speculation." Ulrich's quiet voice pulled their attention. "Let us say there's a warpdrive ship hidden somewhere in the settled galaxy since Earth's twenty-first century tribulations. What brought you to Trinity? What brought you—" He jabbed his finger straight down toward the swirled concrete. "—here?"

Stone smiled. "Now who's acting coy, Mr. Ulrich? That lost warpdrive ship was named *Lady Lux*. We believe it's hidden somewhere in this system. We believe you think so too and you're trying to find it. We know someone with Trinity government connections broke into a UN facility and had opportunity to steal fab plans for spaceship parts. We want to help you build an interplanetary spaceship and find *Lady Lux*."

Ulrich's face, and Laclede's, both betrayed nothing. Ulrich spoke, jutting out fingers with each sentence. "Lost warpdrive ships are something out of an action-adventure movie. No one here has stolen anything from any UN facility. No one here is building an interplanetary spaceship."

"Whatever you say." Stone laughed. His face slowly sobered. "Special Agent Laclede knows that Trinity government agencies have a backdoor to civilian fab logs. He may not know that the UN has backdoors to Trinity government agencies. If you're going to fab anything illicit using either the Trinity police or Ulrich Industrial Equipment fabs in your basement or wherever, first cut their access to the planetary net. And if you're going to illicitly fab an interplanetary spaceship, I have a billion miles more experience piloting a spaceship than everyone else on Trinity put together."

"Assuming all your speculations were true, why would you help us find *Lady Lux*?"

"If the pilot is dead," Stone said, "we want to use *Lady Lux* to perform missionary work. Angela can maintain the warp generators and I should be able to fly it. There are dozens of known colonies, and God alone knows how many unknown ones, that need to hear the Gospel." He rolled his wrists, exposing his palms. "After we fly it on whatever voyage you have planned."

"What if—hypothetically, of course—the pilot were alive?"

"We'd ask him to take us on," Stone said.

Caitlyn added, "If he won't, you could give us false identification and let us settle on Trinity."

Ulrich gave them a last intense look, then glanced at Laclede. The special agent nodded and rose from his armchair. "Mr. and Mrs. Becker, we'll quarter you here in the facility. Stay in your quarters until we come for you."

"How long?" Caitlyn asked.

Laclede approached. "Until we come for you." The uniformed policemen fell into formation around Stone and Caitlyn, guided them to the door.

Stone glanced over his shoulder one last time. Ulrich stood at the picture windows, hands behind his back, looking outward at the lowlands' thick mists.

CHAPTER 10

The apartment stifled Stone with kitschy mass-produced paintings of dismounted cowboys kneeling in prayer beside their horses and wooden chairs with routered knobs and quilted pads tied to hard seats. A kitchenette yielded trays of frozen beef stew, a steamer bag of rolls, and a microwave oven to cook them. The apartment had windows, at least, overlooking the dense clouds covering the lowlands.

The apartment's door was locked from the outside.

In the living room after dinner, Stone picked up from a side table a printed Bible with gold-edged pages, then joined Caitlyn on a sofa facing the windows. He flipped open the Bible and pages crinkled as he turned to a random spot about a third of the way through.

The hand of the Lord was upon me, and carried me out in the spirit of the Lord, and set me down in the midst of the valley which was full of bones, and caused me to pass by them round about: and, behold, there were very many in the open valley; and, lo, they were very dry. And he said unto me, Son of man, can these bones live? And I answered—

Bitch please.

A rocky, sullen feeling formed in his chest. Then the Tobias Becker persona receded from his awareness, leaving him alone with the words of someone as dead as those dry bones for thousands of years.

Somewhere deep in the facility, machinery hummed into action. Something big enough to reverberate through the facility's concrete skeleton.

Caitlyn watched the cloud deck, her knees pulled up to her chest. *What if Ulrich's men don't find our personas in the worldweb?*

She knew tradecraft well enough to assume hidden cameras and microphones monitored them. Good. *Relax. Gray's people gave the Beckers enough of a paper trail to fool them.*

But it won't say the Beckers are UN operat— She let her eyes fall shut, her head loll against her chair's backrest. *Which fits,* she said with more control. *Ulrich and Laclede would expect the UN to scrub the worldweb of any evidence the Beckers are operatives.* She lowered her head to her knees, wrapped her arms around her shins. *But I hate waiting.*

What would the Beckers do? Stone leaned toward her. "We don't have to sit here doing nothing, Angela."

She looked up at him from under an arched eyebrow. "How can you want sex at a time like this?"

Stone raised the Bible from his lap. "I meant we could read scripture together. How could you think I want sex?"

"Because you always want sex when you're stressed. Remember that time in the libertarian colony on the asteroid Pallas—"

"Years ago."

"—that wasn't the only time and you know it."

Stone inhaled. "Alright, yes, I wanted sex when I was stressed. But that was ten years ago. I was trying to distract myself rather than face my problems. I don't want to do that anymore."

She regarded him for a long moment. "You've matured and I haven't noticed."

"I suppose," he said, because no husband, not even a Bible-reading milquetoast like Tobias Becker would tell his wife the truth. Not maturity. He'd just gotten old.

A thought rocked Stone's upper body. It wasn't Tobias Becker who'd gotten old.

It was him.

Caitlyn lowered her knees and turned her torso toward him. She laid her hand on his bare forearm. "Read to me."

He returned his gaze to Ezekiel, chapter 37, and read aloud. "'… And he said unto me, Son of man, can these bones live? And I answered—'" He swallowed dryly. "'O Lord God, thou knowest.'"

"That's the most awe-inspiring passage in the Old Testament," Caitlyn said. From her tone he could almost believe she meant it, instead of parroting the sentiments of the Angela Becker persona.

"You never told me this passage meant so much to you. What makes it so awe-inspiring?"

Caitlyn took a moment. Still learning how to organize a persona's thoughts. "No matter how dire a situation looks, God can reverse it. And Ezekiel knows it to the bottom of his soul."

Hours ticked by. They continued reading the Bible, talking. Stone eventually decided her tone when describing the verse from Ezekiel had simply been good acting. Caitlyn couldn't find any passage from anyone's holy book awe-inspiring. She lived in Manhattan in the twenty-second century of the common era, after all. Working as an undercover operative couldn't move her any further away from religious belief.

Knuckles rapped on the door. Caitlyn started. Stone gently closed the Bible and paced toward the door.

Shouldn't we—? Caitlyn asked. Her gaze jumped around the apartment's living room and open-plan kitchenette.

He'd noticed improvised weapons within five minutes after the Laclede's men locked the door. A chef's knife in the kitchenette. A cross of dense synthwood hanging on the wall. *Head to the kitchen like you're going to offer our visitors a glass of water. Keep your right hand near the knife drawer.*

Caitlyn scurried to the kitchen. "You get the door and I'll see what we can offer our guests to drink."

Stone eyed the eight feet between the door and the wall-mounted cross, then reached for the door's handle. Still locked. "Come on in," he said.

Touchpad buttons beeped. The lock snicked. Outside, a gruff male voice said, "Open when you're ready."

A good sign, but—*Stay alert.* He opened the door.

The same three policemen from earlier waited outside. Different hair and eye colors, but similar broad faces, scowling eyebrows, and scents of hair gels. The one in the middle, his hair auburn and his eyes a deeper brown, said, "Mr. and Mrs. Becker, please come with us."

"What's this about?"

"Mr. Ulrich has some more questions for you both."

"Questions?" Stone checked the platinum hands and silicon wafer face of his wristwatch. Almost ten at night. "It's very late."

"Mr. Ulrich is awake."

"Of course. We need a moment to freshen up. Please, come in."

The policeman shook his wide head. "We'll wait here." He shut the door.

In the kitchen, Caitlyn's slender fingers rested on the knife drawer's handle. *Well?*

They haven't tipped me off to any plans to kill us, Stone replied. He glanced up and down her khaki capris and thin blouse. *Do you have a place to hide a knife?*

No. She drew her hand back from the knife drawer. *We can take these policemen in unarmed combat if we had to.*

Keep that in our back pocket. Now head to the bathroom and make sure the hidden mics pick up the sound of running water.

Three minutes later, they came to an elevator. One of the policeman —black hair, dark eyes with a hint of epicanthic fold—jabbed the button for a lower floor. Stone shared a sidelong glance with Caitlyn. They weren't returning to the lounge where they first met Ulrich, and she knew it too.

A ding and the doors slid open. Another concrete hallway, narrower than the higher ones, adorned only with stark white LEDs. The mechanical hum sounded louder, just a few walls or floors away. The policemen fell in around Stone and Caitlyn, one leading, two following. In formation they strode over rougher concrete, past closed metal doors lacking and light seeping out from under. From ahead came sounds—body movements, indistinct voices, electronic beeps, cooling fans. Some activity took place on this level.

They rounded a corner. On opposite walls, two open doors faced each other, spilling light into the middle of the hallway. Ulrich and Laclede stood there, talking in low tones, while policemen and figures in rumpled dark trousers and blue polo shirts went between the open rooms by circling around Laclede and Ulrich.

"Our guests," Ulrich said. "I trust your quarters were comfortable?"

Caitlyn answered. "Very much."

"The two of you kept busy?"

Stone nodded. "Thank you for providing the Bible in the apartment. I'd almost forgotten how wonderful its pages feel under my fingertips."

"Good." Ulrich glanced at Laclede, then refocused on Stone and Caitlyn. "My people spent the intervening hours verifying your story on the worldweb."

Stone kept his limbs loose. Caitlyn spoke. "We guessed as much."

"The public records confirm your names, educational history, and travels in the outer reaches of Sol System. They're silent regarding your UN affiliation, which we expected."

"We understand you felt the need to do that," Stone said. "Now that we've demonstrated our trustworth—"

Ulrich raised his hand. "The public records confirm your stories, yes. But what confirms the public records?"

Stone squinted. "You sound like a dorm-room atheist who denies the truth of the Bible."

"You met many atheists in the dorms at your Christian university?"

"Believe it or not…." Stone gave his mouth a lopsided quirk.

"Sadly, I believe you." Ulrich's brown eyes intensified the look he gave Stone. "My grandfather told me about the unholy alliances between the US government and the Big Data conglomerates in Silicon Valley. The CEO of Googolbook kneeled before the Whore of Babylon. He gave to her all his data on his billion customers, and to his billion customers he beamed her propaganda."

"I don't follow…." Caitlyn said.

"Special Agent Laclede and I are certain the UN could construct false identities for its spies."

Stone looked quizzical. "You're saying we aren't Tobias and Angela

Becker? We didn't fly a fusion-drive ship around Sol System for a decade?" Then he chuckled. "False identities. You're talking theory. We've seen the UN in practice."

"We don't doubt that," Ulrich said. Laclede's right elbow bent, bringing his hand closer to the pistol hidden under his jacket.

"How many man-hours would just one false identity take to construct and maintain? Then double it. Then add the extra confirming touches—plugging the false identity into social network posts by other people—you saw us tagged by our college friends, didn't you? The pastor who officiated at our wedding?"

"My people did. If your identities are false, their worldweb traces are extremely convincing."

"So what will it take," Stone said, "to convince you?"

Ulrich kept his intense brown eyes locked on Stone. He pointed at the open door to his right. "In there, Ms. Becker. And, Mr. Becker...." Ulrich pointed to the other door, to his left.

Stone glanced from Ulrich to Laclede. From their stony faces, the colonials had decided to test Stone and Caitlyn before the policemen knocked on the apartment door, and nothing would change their minds.

He shrugged, then said to Caitlyn, "See you in a few." He moved in, past fragrant blond strands, toward her full lips. She leaned into his kiss. Her lips were warm against his.

Stone pulled back soon. *Had to sell it.*

I know. She went around Stone toward her assigned door. Then he strode to his.

A windowless room, concrete floor and gypsum board walls, as soulless as the twenty-first century classroom buildings on the NYU campus. Inside, power and data cables dangled from the backs of six computer displays. The displays hung on a metal frame jutting up from the edge of a synthwood table. They formed a solid bank of screens three wide and two high. The outermost displays angled inward and the upper three angled down. Each of the six aimed at the same spot hidden from the door.

At that spot, Stone would take his test.

CHAPTER 11

To Stone's left, the wheels of a roller stool squeaked. From behind the bank of displays showed a male head, disheveled brown hair and soft eyes. "Mr. Becker?" he said in a voice higher than Stone expected. "I'm Carter."

Living in Manhattan gave Stone a well-tuned gaydar. Carter would suffer if his sexual orientation came out to religious fanatics like Ulrich. Stone filed the insight away for future use, if needed. "What can I do for you?"

"Please, come, have a seat." Carter wheeled his stool backward, flourished his hand toward the spot the displays aimed at.

Stone did as the other man bade. He rounded the corner of the display bank. On the far side, angled toward the seat, the top display showed six zones lined with alphanumerics. The display below showed a fisheye view of a black circle. A faint halo of light and incomplete shadow ringed the circle and hinted the dark middle obscured a deep parabolic pit.

The other displays held more windows of text, more camera views. Deep blue sky dabbed with puffy white clouds. Panoramas of a broad tarmac interspersed with pits, and watched by distant, windowless buildings. A feed from a remote camera showed the ship, poking its nose above a matte gray donut of a gantry. The gantry's base obscured the ship's launch pit from view.

Stone's peripheral vision hinted at what rested on the tabletop in front of the monitor bank. A focused glance confirmed a wide control panel of switches, illuminator diodes, and six sliders. Old tech, compared to the Becker persona's memory of piloting by a bulky, heavy transcranial stim helmet. But Becker went through hundreds of hours of simulator time, hands on controls like these, to earn his license. The needed skills would flow from his brain to his fingers.

He went to a chair of plastic black mesh and rested his hand atop the backrest, next to a headset and attached microphone splayed on the chair. Stone kept his face blank while glee spiked inside his chest. Ulrich and Laclede had guessed the UN could construct a doc trail for a cover identity.

They had no idea a UN operative could speedlearn the skills to back that cover identity up.

They're going to have me pilot a spaceflight sim, he subvoked to Caitlyn. *You?*

She took a moment to reply and sounded hurried. *Explain exotic matter physics. Can't talk more.*

"Are you ready, Mr. Becker?" Carter asked.

Stone panned his gaze over the monitor display. "What's the scenario?"

"Launch from an Earth-like world on a braki—bratchi?"

"Brachistochrone. With a *k* sound."

"Let's call it a direct trajectory to one of its moons," Carter said. "A captured asteroid. Close within 2000 meters and hold station."

Stone tightened his grip on the backrest. "I never launched from Earth. I flew our ship between space stations and asteroids, mostly. The heaviest place we took off from was Europa. A moon of Jupiter. About one-eighth *g*." To his own ears, his voice held just enough unease to make believable that he was a good pilot but knew his limitations.

"You have closer experience to this scenario than anyone else on Trinity." Carter's voice took on a plaintive edge. "Please don't let us down."

Let *Carter* down? Failure at this simulator scenario meant, at best, a desperate fight out of the facility and across sixty miles of hostile terrain to the wormhole. At worst, a bullet to the brain and a burial under the lowland's incessant cloudbank.

Stone sat and spun the black mesh chair to face the monitor bank. Reached behind himself for the headset, put it on his ears, swung the microphone near his mouth. Tobias Becker's false memories of the cockpit of his ship nudged at Stone's awareness, flavoring his thoughts as he ran through the pre-flight checklist speedlearned by his brain.

His gaze darted to the displays, his hands rocked switches.

*Drive 1 fuel level ok.

Drive 1 diagnostic.

Drive 2 fuel level ok.

Drive 2 diagnostic.

Drive 1 diagnostic ok.

Initiate drive 1 pre-flight....*

A low hum reached his ears. The hum incremented a tiny amount as he proceeded through the checklist.

....Initiate drive 6 pre-flight.

He activated the ship-wide comm channel. "All personnel, strap in for launch in 30 seconds." The lower right monitor showed a ship's perspective-view schematic of cylindrical decks peopled with a dozen red, human-shaped icons. Within five seconds, most turned yellow.

Stone turned to an alphanumerics overlay on the lower left monitor. Ambient conditions for the sim: 114° F, 28.6 psi, 0.84 g.

Ulrich had picked those ambient conditions for a damn good reason.

Stone rocked the master drive switch to *standby* and the slider controller to *unison*. He shoved the master drive slider past eighteen, about halfway to maximum. The other five followed. With an eye on the display panel, he adjusted the drives to 18.400 m/s^2. Indicator icons glowed green.

More green glowed in the lower right monitor: the twelve human shapes, overlaid with icons of five-point harnesses.

His fingers paused at the master drive switch. Rocked it to *active.*

Intense brightness swamped the rear camera view. Software dimmed the camera feed, but still the torrent of energized exhaust flooding from the drives dazzled Stone's eyes. More software kept the engine roar in his headphones to a safe level.

The panorama display showed the tarmac falling away. Bright needles of light merged into a single intense pillar in the external as the ship cleared the donut-shaped gantry.

All systems looked good. Stone mashed his lips between his teeth. His fingers rested on the control board. In Ulrich and Laclede's shoes, he would order Carter to program the sim to throw a serious, but solvable, error at Tobias Becker....

The external view vanished. A nav display took its place. The limb of the 'Earth-like world' occupied one corner, and in the opposite corner, a blow-up circle centered on a tumbling rock about 300,000 miles away. A glowing yellow dot on the planet's surface marked the ship. Alphanumerics showed net acceleration, current velocity, and current distance to the turnover point halfway to the target rock.

The drives continued to roar. A metallic clang sounded, but not in Stone's headphones. Some activity nearby in the facility.

He blinked away the distraction. The clouds in the forward view grew larger, then smaller. The sky turned darker and darker, going from deep blue to black. Two crosshairs appeared, a red one in the middle of the view, a yellow one slightly off center. A memory of peering downrange through a sniper scope, waiting for an eastern European politician to step out of a hotel, clashed with Stone's speedlearned skills.

Stone blinked. The yellow crosshairs marked the target rock. His fingers rolled a trackball on the panel until both sets of crosshairs lined up. A cheerful ping sounded in the headphones. He flicked the automatic attitude control system switch on, then spoke a command to be alerted if fuel for attitude control dropped to 60%. He could always draw hydrogen pellets from the main drive tanks, but so much better if you can avoid it....

Current velocity kept climbing. Net acceleration—the 18.400 m/s^2 supplied by the drives minus the planet's gravitational force—ticked up by a millimeter per second-squared. The planet's gravitational pull on the ship would drop rapidly as the ship proceeded—*inverse square laws, activate!* rose from Tobias Becker on a bubble of nerdish pride.

Nudge the master drive slider down every tenth of a *gee* and none of the passengers would notice.

A speedlearned hunch gave him an estimate of the time to turnover even before a glance at an alphanumeric provided an exact number. 7005 seconds, 7004, 7003…. a hair under two hours. Then double it for the deceleration leg and add a few minutes to fine tune the ship's position at the target.

Would they make him run the sim till two in the morning?

A window popped up, mirrored on all six monitors, answering his question. *Quick time available. 2x. 4x. 8x. Dismiss.*

"Four-x," he spoke to the microphone. A clock icon, along with the changing velocity and range-to-target alphanumerics, picked up speed. A few seconds later he nudged the master drive slider down. Over the next thirty minutes he made dozens more nudges, faster and faster, as the ship gained speed and moved further from the planet's center of mass. The glare of drive exhaust in the rear camera view lessened enough for him to see. Net acceleration remained within a few decimal points of 10 m/s^2. Close enough to 1 g for the passengers to imagine they were on Earth. Easy.

Too easy.

The nav display showed the ship would reach the turnover point in a minute. Stone checked the internal schematic. Eleven of the dozen passenger icons showed the harness overlay. Most green, three yellow, showing they'd pulled objects out of storage. The twelfth icon occupied the lavatory on C deck. Alone? No one on Trinity would want to join the million-mile-high club?

A smirk twisted his face. Carter had coded a family-friendly sim.

He activated the ship-wide comm channel. "All personnel, we will enter free-fall in forty-five seconds. Return to your seats as soon as possible. Stow all loose objects and strap in. The longer you take, the harder we'll have to burn to decelerate to target."

The twelfth icon soon left the lavatory. The icons turned green and strapped in.

Where would the trick come? Stone glanced at the displays. Over 95% fuel remained in the attitude control tanks. No trick there. He reached for the master drive slider without looking. Turnover in 3, 2, 1—

He shut down the drives in one smooth motion. His stomach flopped from the Becker persona's expectation of free-fall. The drive exhaust glare vanished. The blue-green disc of the launch planet, about as wide as a thumb held at arm's length, appeared in empty space against a backdrop of stars. In the displays, net acceleration dropped to zero. Velocity held constant at about 70 klicks per second.

"Give me a decel attitude target."

White crosshairs appeared over the blue-green disc, like a sniper scope targeting a planet. Stone turned off the automatic attitude control system. Spun the trackball. The red crosshairs slid left across the forward view, down the starfield in the port side panorama, and from the right edge of the rear view toward the white crosshairs. He stopped the red crosshairs one pixel short of perfect alignment, then turned automatic attitude control back on.

"Starting deceleration," he said over the ship-wide channel, "in 5, 4, 3, 2, 1." He slid the master drive up to 10.000 m/s^2. The current velocity decremented. Easy.

Too easy.

Somewhere nearby in the facility, pumps chugged.

For the next twenty-five minutes, the ship's velocity crept downward. Software overlaid the red crosshairs marking the target rock on the drive glare filling the rear camera. The red crosshairs hung barely off-center.

Barely, but still too far off center, he realized two hundred kilometers, about three minutes, away from the target rock. His darting eyes scanned the displays. Attitude control still on automatic.

Now came the test within the test.

"Run diagnostics on attitude control." Twelve small drives, arranged in rings of four at the front, middle, and rear of the ship. One of them malfunctioned, running a little hot or cold, pushing the ship off its intended flight path. The diagnostics would identify the drive and its problem. A quick command would either run a self-repair routine on the defective drive or tell the attitude control system to recalibrate around the defect.

Up popped a window. *Attitude control system ok. AC drives 1-12 ok.* The hell?

A smirk touched Stone's lips. The program simulated a malfunction undetectable by the diagnostics. A clever trick.

His mouth felt dry. How to solve it? Keep tapping the attitude control trackball? Or—

Caitlyn's voice burst into his hearing. *I just spent an hour talking about exotic matter—*

No time! He cut the connection. Where was he? Attitude control malfunction.

Stone breathed in. His smirk returned. His objective was to hold station at 2000 meters from the target rock. He didn't have to hold station alongside the target....

ETA 150 seconds, range 112 km. Bump the deceleration by a small amount and the ship would stop 2000 meters short. A small boost, unnoticeable by the passengers. Speedlearned intuitions flowed from his brain through his fingers. He bumped the master drive slider to $10.18 \, \text{m/s}^2$.

The ETA timer replaced the digits with hyphens. The range and velocity shrank as the simulated seconds ticked by. "All personnel, prepare for free fall." Green icons bloomed in the corner of his eye. One last tweak to drive output. Wait for the exact moment—

Stone swept the master drive slider to zero. The display showed velocity 0 m/s, range 1998.71 m. He flicked the *hold station* switch, then leaned his head back. He slipped the headphones off, tossed them over a hook mounted on the control panel. He gave Carter a cocky smirk, with just a touch of butch flirtation. "Anything else?"

"No," Carter said, awe and longing tinging his voice. "Wait here. Please." The stool's wheels squeaked on the concrete floor. Soft footsteps padded out of the room.

Stone sniffed out a chuckle. He could wrap Carter around his finger if he needed to later in the mission. He subvoked to Caitlyn, *I passed. Did you?*

What do you think?

He sniffed out a breath. *You're pissy all of a sudden. Mad I cut you off a minute ago?*

She didn't reply. Answering his question with *yes*.

Before he could call her out on losing focus, three sets of footsteps came through the door. Stone knew whom the footsteps belonged to before Ulrich, Laclede, and Carter came around the corner of the display bank.

He stood up to meet them. "How did I do?"

Ulrich regarded him with intense brown eyes. "Better than I expected. How many years has it been since you've flown an interplanetary ship?"

A shrug. "Like riding a bike," Stone said.

"No doubt." Ulrich glanced at Laclede from under raised eyebrows. The tall bald man replied with a minuscule nod and Ulrich returned his gaze to Stone. "Follow us."

Stone left the room behind the two of them. Carter fell in next to him, a puppy-dog look in his eyes. He wanted Stone to pilot a ship? Kiss him? Both?

They crossed the hall, entered the other room. Smartboards along the wall bore equations and sketches, all limned by a precise, feminine hand.

"Angela?" Stone asked. Carter's face fell.

Caitlyn unfolded long legs and rose from a spindly chair of molded yellow plastic. To two men seated near her, she said, "Dr. Chen, Dr. Sanders, my husband, Tobias."

After handshakes, the younger man—Sanders, who looked more like a baseball player than a physicist, and smelled of citrusy cologne— said, "Your wife is a remarkable woman."

"I've known that for years," Stone said.

Chuckles from the scientists. Sanders' gaze shifted to Ulrich and Laclede. "An excellent set of talents and skills."

"Noted," Ulrich said. He and Laclede muttered to one another.

As the two colonists talked, Caitlyn put on a sweet smile, belied by the sarcastic tone of her next subvoked words to Stone. *You're piling it on thick.*

Praising Angela is in character for Tobias.

But not for you. Don't try to flatter me. You were still rude to cut me off—

Stone's next words sounded gruff. *Head in the game, keyhole kop.*

I'm a professional.

Ulrich and Laclede's body language shifted. Closed eyes, bowed heads. Ulrich murmured a prayer. They looked to have reached a decision and wanted divine blessing on it. *You better be.*

"…Amen. Angela. Tobias." Ulrich's voice compelled attention from everyone in the room. "You have both proven yourselves. As you have guessed, we believe the lost warpdrive ship is somewhere in Trinity system. Please help us find it."

Caitlyn smiled. "We're glad to—"

"—help," Stone said, "but remember, if the pilot is dead, we want to use it to spread the Gospel."

Ulrich's brown eyes narrowed, but the intense fervor in them burned through. "Fly one mission for us, Mr. and Mrs. Becker, and the warpdrive ship shall be yours."

CHAPTER 12

The hum of truck engines echoed through the cavernous garage. Eight rigs in column, hitched to flatbed trailers holding spaceship parts. Curving slabs of hull stacked on a truck near the front. The drive nozzles further back. All uncovered.

Why didn't Ulrich and Laclede conceal the spaceship parts from prying eyes? Did they want to get caught? Or did they think they could build and launch the ship before UN personnel could stop them? Unlikely....

Stone set the question aside and reviewed the rest of the column. A tanker, frosty with condensation and covered like a lamppost with warning signs for purified liquid hydrogen. A mobile command center in an enclosed trailer. Hummvees at point and tail. Every vehicle was matte-black with a faceted radar-disrupting body.

Workers lined up to board a bus halfway down the column. Ulrich and Laclede strode past them, toward the front. The workers gave Stone and Caitlyn the same awestruck looks they'd received upstairs.

Laclede opened the door of the lead hummvee. His long arm beckoned Caitlyn and Stone in.

"Take the rear seats," Ulrich said from outside.

They climbed in. An extended cabin, with room for six, behind the driver's seat. The driver chewed on his bushy mustache, the rest of his face obscured by a comm helmet. The driver drummed his fingers on the steering wheel.

A gigantic rumble sounded nearby, heavy enough to rattle the synthetic leather under Stone's butt.

He looked past the driver and out the windshield. His eyebrows darted up.

Ulrich and Laclede took the rear-facing seats in the front. Ulrich's humorless brown eyes glinted at Stone. "You knew our destination from the sim, I should think."

Mouth gaping, eyes slowly blinking, Stone said, "I didn't know how we would get there."

The rumble stopped. In front of the hummvee, hidden armatures held aloft a section of the concrete wall twenty feet wide and high. A dark circle flat on the bottom—a tunnel mouth—gaped in the exposed face of gray-brown rock. A reflective strip inside the tunnel curved left and angled downward.

"The tunnel was the most challenging thing to keep secret," Ulrich said. "Three years to excavate a switchbacking ramp gentle enough for trucks to descend to the lowlands. The first four months, the cuttings had to be disposed over the plateau's edge outside the notice of your former employers—and our own personnel who lacked need-to-know. Eventually we reached a depth where we could build side tunnels under the cloud bank and dispose of cuttings directly from the tunnel."

"Power consumption must have been high, too," Caitlyn said.

"Very perceptive, Mrs. Becker. We fabbed a fusion reactor specifically to power the project and diverted a nearby stream to provide hydrogen fuel. Keeping that secret added to the challenge."

Stone frowned. "Three years to build, you said? When did UNAIM set up shop on Trinity?"

"After we started."

"You started building the tunnel before you knew you could get plans for spaceship parts?"

"I assigned engineers to design a spaceship and fab its parts. We would have completed the project eventually. UNAIM's inept security made our task easier."

The driver cleared his throat. "All vehicles report ready, sir."

Ulrich looked to Laclede, Stone, and Caitlyn in turn. "There is a time to prepare, and a time to act." He raised his voice to the driver. "Proceed."

The driver tapped buttons on a touchscreen. The hummvee rolled into the tunnel mouth. The headlights snapped on. Reflective strips lining the tunnel glowed, then dissipated into the vast darkness ahead.

Caitlyn's hazel eyes peered out the windows at rock faces lit sidelong by the headlights of trailing trucks. A pipe running parallel to the roadway sprouted sprinkler heads like mushrooms. "How long is the tunnel?"

"Fifty miles," Ulrich replied. "The engineers recommended no more than a 10% grade to ensure the trucks remain under control. We'll emerge in an hour and forty minutes."

Monotonous gray and brown rock walls on either hand. Stone leaned back his head, yawned wide-mouthed to equalize the pressure in his ears, shut his eyes. He followed by sound what the others did. Ulrich breathed slowly. Meditating, perhaps. Wait, he would call it praying. Near Ulrich, khaki rustled. Laclede crossing his legs. Next to Stone, Caitlyn's breathing slowed. Ready to fake sleep as a cover for subvoking? She'd better not. If Laclede's men picked up wireless signals emanating from inside the cabin…. then she snored through a sharp left turn and continuing descent.

An early morning followed by a late night, but still, she shouldn't really fall asleep. Maybe she'd lain awake the previous night, tossing and turning about their kiss outside the test rooms and what it meant.

Not the first time he'd affected women that way.

Stone eased his head into the headrest, slowed his breathing. By now, Ulrich and Laclede should believe he was asleep. Maybe they would talk to each other and reveal something. Unlikely—the tunnel's construction proved they knew how to play the game. Silence ruled the hummvee's cabin.

His head sank deeper. Images of the spaceship sim formed in Stone's mind's eye….

He woke with pressure in his ears. He shut his mouth, pinched his nose shut, pushed air out of his lungs until his ears popped.

Then he noticed the hummvee drove on level ground. Outside the windows stretched a rocky terrain, barely glimpsed in the scattered light of the truck headlights behind them. The lowlands of Trinity. Clouds hung low, so dense they blocked almost all of Bethany's reflected light. Based on Gray's briefing, there would be nothing but rock, scoured by wind and rain, between the plateau and whatever fungi scummed the coast. Impossible to live off the land, if he and Caitlyn had to flee from the launch site. Impossible to steal a vehicle and drive up the tunnel, into the muzzles of police guns.

They had to play their roles until the fall of the final curtain.

Ulrich pressed the standby switch on his tablet's bezel, then turned his brown eyes to Stone. "Another hour until we get to the launch site. The workers will need eight to ten hours to assemble and run diagnostics on the ship."

Stone's mind switched gears. "When do we launch?"

Ulrich's gaze intensified. "Immediately after construction."

"If you give me a tablet, I'll work on a launch trajectory to avoid detection—"

"I will, and feel free to do so, but Carter already booted up the ship's nav computer and instructed it to launch on an angle to minimize visibility to the plateau."

Stone angled his head. "Are you certain you can trust him?"

"He's been with us four years," Laclede said coldly. "You've been with us less than a day."

"Come now," Ulrich said. His quiet voice was a dagger of reproach. "The Beckers have proven themselves already. Soon they will prove themselves even more."

"Rest assured of that," Stone said, "but that's not what I meant. He doesn't have any experience in space travel. I was a pilot for over a decade."

A confident smile formed on Ulrich's mouth. "I'll review both your trajectory and Carter's before we launch." Next to him on the front seat, Laclede gave Stone an unreadable look through sunken eyes.

Earlier, Ulrich's men must have bulldozed the track the hummvee followed. Mounds of loose rocks flanked a trail of smooth rock fifteen yards wide. Smeared blobs of black paint criss-crossed the trail. The hummvee's headlights revealed deep textures in the paint blobs, which growled under the vehicle's tires. Chaff to fool any UN radars that might be aimed down through the clouds.

Every tenth of a mile, transponder beacons jutted out of the mounds. Vertical reflector strips glowed on the beacons' sides. Channelized by the transponders, the hummvee drove itself forward. The driver looked to be a precaution in case they had to leave the trail.

Caitlyn's voice flowed through the dim cabin. "I've been wondering for a while, Mr. Ulrich. Do you know where in Trinity's system *Lady Lux* is hidden?"

"Yes. Bethany's next moon out. Gethsemane."

"Is Gethsemane visible from Anderson City?" Stone asked.

Ulrich's arched eyebrow answered before his low voice said, "No."

Of course not. Ulrich and Laclede hadn't spent years prepping a hidden launch in order to streak a fusion exhaust tail across the sky in view of the UN. Skillful players, just like his most recent opponent, though they played a different game than Teresa Benavides had on Freeland. "I'll need Gethsemane's current location to lay in a course. In case Carter's computer malfunctions."

"The tablet will include astrogation data," Ulrich said. "I trust the eight hours required by the workmen will give you enough time for all your needed calculations?"

"More than enough," Stone said.

The hummvee rolled on between transponders. The driver swiped the screen of a tablet mounted in the middle of the dashboard. Reading a book.

"How do you know *Lady Lux* is on Gethsemane?" Caitlyn asked the men across the cabin.

"You're rather curious," Laclede said coldly.

"I want to know the story, so that Tobias and I may tell it to the souls we bring to Christ, if we can use the ship to serve the Lord."

Laclede's sunken eyes gave her a flat look.

Ulrich smiled a thin-lipped smile. "A commendable request. We will tell you. Special Agent Laclede?"

"Me?"

"God led you to the file, not me."

Laclede shrugged. "Your grandfather had it—"

"And I would never have found it on my own. Tell them."

"Alright. I was investigating the—death—of Mr. Ulrich's grandfather—"

Ulrich's quiet voice corrected. "He was murdered."

Laclede pressed his lips together, a sign he doubted Ulrich's assertion. "He died right after the ITB scout ship found Trinity. The UN officials had made their pitch. More wealth and power for Trinity's leaders. They only had to give a fraction of the plateau to refugees from Earth's conflict zones. Only a few refugees, not enough to change our culture. They'd even ensure the only refugees were Christians."

"Go on," Caitlyn said.

"Mr. Ulrich's grandfather was an adamant opponent of the UN's offer. He was a founder, born on Earth during the Time of Troubles. He knew what UN refugees meant. Whether those refugees professed Christ or not." Laclede's voice tightened. "The younger leaders—"

"Speak frankly," Ulrich said. "My father was a traitor to our people. I've known for over half my life."

"—Mr. Ulrich's father and the other younger leaders saw only the benefits to them, not the costs to Trinity as a whole. So, when Mr. Ulrich's grandfather died suddenly, we had to rule out assassination."

The hummvee dipped, then forded a stream on a slab of concrete, a low-water bridge. Water splashed against the tires. Embedded chaff growled under them.

"I was a young agent then," Laclede said, "so my superiors assigned me to the boring work of digging through the deceased's electronic files and physical effects. Mr. Ulrich's grandfather had a locked safe in his office. I found the combination on a slip of paper in his desk drawer. Inside the safe was a paper file."

A final splash and the hummvee drove onto dry, rocky ground. "Turns out the pilot of *Lady Lux* fled Earth when the UN took over the exotic matter factory. He knew they would come looking for him and he wanted a place to hide. His ship contained a coldsleep tank—"

Caitlyn angled her head at Stone. Her eyebrows arched over glinting hazel eyes.

Stone swatted her upper arm with the back of his hand. They returned their attention to Laclede.

"—an icy body he could melt into with his fusion exhaust to hide from visual and radar detection. Gethsemane was the closest such body to Trinity."

With the Becker persona's help, Stone visualized it. A ship hovering over the iceball moon Gethsemane, with just enough thrust aimed downward to cancel out Gethsemane's gravitational attraction. A melting, boiling pool of ices—mostly water, dry ice, and methane—forming where the drive's fusion exhaust touched the surface. The ship cutting power, sinking into the pool. A trickle of heat coming from the reactor powering the ship's interior, but only a trickle, not enough to keep the pool liquid. The pilot climbing into the coldsleep chamber as the ices refroze—

Look for a patch of smooth ice on Gethsemane's far surface, and you'll find *Lady Lux*.

"How long did he plan to hide?" Caitlyn asked.

"Until we decided we needed him."

Stone said, "When did you decide that?"

"I didn't." Laclede straightened his shoulders. "I slipped that file out of the deceased's office and secured it where only I could access it. From reading the file, I knew we had to resist the UN; but I also knew I couldn't let anyone else discover its existence. Which also meant the pro-UN faction got its way and we got stuck with a million resettled."

Caitlyn winced in the dim light. "Mr. Ulrich, did you know about the file?"

"While my grandfather was alive, you mean? No. I was a boy of fifteen when he was murdered. He knew my heart aligned with his regarding the UN problem. He would have shared the file with me after I matured more, had he lived. God did the next best thing by entrusting the file to Special Agent Laclede until four years ago, after my father died. We met at the funeral, in fact. I sensed immediately—it could only have been the hand of the Lord guiding me—that I could trust Special Agent Laclede with my heart's assessment of my father.

Within weeks, the Lord guided him to share the secret of the file. Together we decided we needed *Lady Lux* once more."

Maybe now Ulrich would let slip his plan. "Why?" Stone asked.

"To undertake the mission God has called on me to lead."

"Which is?"

Though dim light suffused the hummvee's cabin, Ulrich's intense gaze landed on Stone like a weight. "You will know in due time, Mr. Becker. In due time."

CHAPTER 13

The trucks and other vehicles idled in a circle sixty yards across, headlights aimed in at the ship in the center. Like a giant's keg, the ship was a stout cylinder, twenty yards high and fifteen in diameter, resting on four landing struts. Thanks to the Becker persona, Stone read the ship's interior schematics from glances at and under the bright white diamondoid alloy hull. Five drives arranged like the pips of a die. Hydrogen tanks around the perimeter for radiation shielding. A retractable ladder surrounded by a padded safety cage ran up the side, with a horizontal spur to a hinged panel covering a cargo airlock. One airlock for personnel out of sight, maybe atop the ship, leading into workrooms and crew quarters more compressed than a submarine's.

A dozen workers scurried around the ship. Diagnostic tools blinked and beeped in their hands.

If all the workers were coming along, the ship's living space would be as crowded as the cars of resettled on the train from Sarawak.

Ulrich's head jerked. His gaze scanned text inside his eyeglass displays, then he refocused on Caitlyn and Stone. A crisp nod. "All systems pass check. Time to board."

Stone and the two colonial men gestured for Caitlyn to go first up the ladder. Ulrich followed, Laclede behind him, Stone in the rear. Their shoes rang on the ladder. Truck headlights cast shadows of padded safety bars onto the rungs. Stone opened his mouth to the thick lowland air. He emerged onto the top of the ship breathing easily. They all did, even Carter, whom Stone would guess had the worst cardiovascular condition of them all.

"You see the hatch," Ulrich said.

Caitlyn nodded. Glowing paint marked a path to an open airlock at the centerpoint. Up here, where the ship's sides blocked the truck headlights, light from inside the ship glowed against the dense darkness.

She led the way across a spongy black surface, a sacrificial gel that would protect the ship against micrometeorites in flight. At the airlock, she turned and backed down a ladder. The men followed, down through the airlock's open inner hatch, into the control chamber.

Movies made ship interiors seem as spacious as luxury apartments. The Becker persona prepared Stone for the reality before his feet hit the deck. The control chamber might be larger than his closet back home. From the ceiling, off-white LED bulbs bathed the space in harsh light and plunged Laclede's sunken eyes into deep shadow. The four of them crowded together, sleeves brushing. Ulrich's breath, garlicky from a pull-tab-to-heat dinner, made Stone wince. Laclede ducked his bald head under the mass of pipes and hardware housings jutting from the ceiling.

A pocket door slid back behind Laclede. Carter poked his head through. "Sorry about the tight fit." His soft gaze landed on Stone's face, then skittered away.

"Discomfort in doing the Lord's work is no discomfort at all," Ulrich said. "Join us."

Carter squeezed in between Stone and Laclede. He smelled nervous, but not enough to smother Ulrich's garlic breath.

"Your flight plan is ready?" Ulrich said.

A frantic nod tossed Carter's bangs. "I fed all the data to the nav computer—"

"I'm certain. Send it to me." Ulrich angled his head toward Stone. "Both of you."

Carter turned his soft eyes on Stone. His tone held a dissonant mix of surprise, disappointment, relief. "You prepared one too?"

"I've laid in dozens of flight plans. And no computer would have solved the problems you threw into the simulation." Stone reached for the loaner tablet stuck to his hip. Hook-and-loop fabric scritched apart. He iconized the flight plan the Becker persona had coded for him, found Ulrich's local drop icon, and flicked the flight plan to him.

"Carter, you have a holographic display in here?" Ulrich asked. "Ah, I see it. Clone display."

A swirling ball, yellow-orange on one side and dark gray on the other, popped into view. Too big, too close in the cramped room.

Stone leaned his head back. The ball showed finer details now. On the dark side, just below the equator, a fleck of brown tinged with green and dotted with a few pinpoints of light showed through the swirls. The plateau. A pulsing red dot under the clouds between the plateau and the equator was the launch site.

"Zoom out," Ulrich said.

The holographic image of Trinity shrank. A spherical outline formed around it and the rate of shrinkage slowed. A scale multiplier popped up. 1x, 2x… 5x.

A second spherical outline formed, over two feet away. The second scale multiplier read 50x. Inside the second outline hung a dirty white sphere crazed with fine cracks, like a cue ball aged for ten thousand vape-filled nights. Gethsemane, currently 800,000 miles away.

Suddenly, a yellow line erupted from the pulsing red dot on Trinity. The line curled away from the plateau, over the equator and Trinity's north pole, slowly gaining altitude as it went. Past Trinity's north pole, the yellow line straightened, leaving the planet behind. The tip of the yellow line sped up until it was halfway to Gethsemane, then slowed as it approached the icy moon. Travel time six hours, twenty-one minutes.

The yellow line then wrapped around Gethsemane, fifteen miles above the frozen surface. The flight path coiled around the icy moon like a spooling yellow string. Tobias Becker's satisfaction stirred within Stone.

"Thank you, Carter," Ulrich said. "Now we'll look at Mr. Becker's flight plan."

Stone blinked. "It'll be about the same."

A green line from the launch site followed the curve of Trinity's northern hemisphere. Not green. Blue. Stone's proposed trajectory overlapped the nav computer's flight plan so closely in the first thousand miles that the holographic display blended the colors. By the time Stone's trajectory overflew Trinity's north pole, the lines had diverged by a hairsbreadth, Stone's blue a few miles closer to the surface than Carter's yellow—

"Why is your flight path lower?" Ulrich asked. His tone sounded casual. Sounded.

Stone pretended not to hear Ulrich's tone, and replied as if he took the question at face value. "The scenario forced me into a trade-off. A steeper climb would have reduced atmospheric drag, but a greater risk of visibility from the plateau when we first break through the cloud bank. I weighed the options differently than the nav computer did."

"I see." Ulrich seemed to forget the words as he spoke them. His gaze intensified on the holographic display.

The blue line swept across the display, diverged from the yellow. Acceleration at one gee, turnover at the midpoint, deceleration into Gethsemane orbit. The blue line wound around the target moon, trailing green slivers across the yellow coil.

"Hologram off," Ulrich said. The glowing worlds and flight paths vanished, leaving only tired faces lined by the overhead lights. "Carter, well done, but we'll go with Mr. Becker's flight plan."

Tension bled from Carter's shoulders. "That's a great idea, sir."

"Mr. Becker, prepare for launch. I'll order the workers to vacate the blast zone. Half a mile should do?"

"It should," Stone said, "but in Sol System, the standard minimum radius from a planetary launch site is 2000 yards."

"Sol System is ruled by the Whore of Babylon. Half a mile." The intense look in Ulrich's brown eyes softened. "We'll give you space to work—"

Laclede cleared his throat. "Carter should assist Mr. Becker."

"A good point," Ulrich said. "Mr. Becker?"

Stone shrugged. A glance at Laclede's sunken eyes showed the special agent didn't trust him. He worried a UN operative might crash the ship on launch? Foolish, but Stone would put his worries to ease. "Sure." To Carter, he said, "Let's get started."

The others left. Stone looked around the control chamber. Instead of the simulator's massive control panel full of switches and sliders, the ship's controls consisted of two tablets on articulated telescoping arms. A parabolic mic clung like to the corner of each tablet. Voice command inputs.

Stone flipped down the pilot's jump seat, buckled the five-point harness, swung the tablets close to his hands.

On the opposite wall, Carter sat at the copilot's station and buckled himself in with clumsy fingers. Finally, he pulled the copilot's tablet away from the wall. He gave Stone a sheepish look. "Sorry I took so long."

"I was clumsy my first time, too," Stone said. He put just enough of a hint in his words that Carter might fantasize about a double meaning of *first time*. "Sit back and watch."

The Becker persona flowed into the muscles of his head, upper torso, and arms. Stone resisted for a moment, then let go. He rode the Becker persona, unaware of his fingers' flight over the tablet screens, his voice's muttered gibberish. Time seemed unreal. People dissolved into abstract icons on the maps of the ship and the launch site. The ship and all its systems filled his imagination—the hum of ventilation, the pungent stink from the head, the bitter cold of hydrogen pellets pinging off the fuel tank walls.

From time to time Carter asked questions. Stone answered with distracted monosyllables. Back to what mattered. Systems checks, laying in the flight path—a spike of annoyance when Carter accessed it, but Stone quashed it. Carter did the job Laclede ordered. Stone would never fault a man for following orders. Of course, he might kill a man for doing so....

The Becker persona grumbled. Stone had entered a wrong target deceleration for the insertion into Gethsemane orbit. He corrected it with firm taps on the right-hand tablet. Not a problem, the nav computer would have checked his numbers and suggested a correction—

Trust your God-given talent before you trust a machine bubbled up from the Becker persona.

Stone shook his head, then plunged back into flight prep. So deeply that at one point he glanced up and blinked at limp brown bangs and eyes guarding a secret. Carter. He'd forgotten the colonial had remained in the control chamber.

"Learning anything so far?" Stone asked.

Carter lurched back. "Oh, yes, of course, I…. Was I tapping the screen too hard?" he blurted. "I didn't mean to distract you."

"You didn't." Stone's attention already turned away from Carter, back to the flight prep checklist unreeling before his eyes. Just twenty minutes more and the ship would be ready for launch.

CHAPTER 14

A smooth, synthetic female voice spoke over the internal comm channel. "...3 ...2 ...1 ...ignition."

The fusion drives rumbled deep in the ship. Three gees pulled Stone's arms away from the *Launch sequenced commenced* popup on the dangling tablets, squashed his body into the jump seat. He pushed out his chest and abdomen, fighting for the stream of oxygen flowing through his face mask. Over the bass roar of the drives, his breaths resounded in the helmet securing his head and neck against whiplash.

And unlike a sharp turn or jackrabbit start in a racing car, the acceleration forces didn't let up. Traversing the wormhole by car or train hadn't prepared him for this. The simulation at Ulrich and Laclede's secret facility hadn't prepared him for this. But thanks to the Becker persona, he could speak over the comm channel with aplomb. "All good? Speak, don't nod."

Caitlyn and the men from Trinity sat on jump seats around control room. Caitlyn to Stone's right, Ulrich and Laclede to his left.

"Feels like our heaviest launch ever," she said.

"By far," Stone said. "Five times heavier than Luna."

"Discomfort is transient," Ulrich said. "The will of the Lord transcends all."

Laclede's voice sounded tight. "I'm fine."

In the jump seat on the far wall, Carter's breaths sounded quick and ragged. "My gosh, my gosh. I'll make it, but my gosh…."

On the tablet screens, an icon of the ship progressed along the flight path. As the ship's trajectory flattened, it tilted forward like an amusement park ride suspending its passengers in mid-air. The five-point harness dug into Stone's chest. Carter gasped and breathed even faster.

In one corner of the displays, traces spasmed back and forth around horizontal lines. A turbulence detector, gauging how much the dense atmosphere buffetted the ship. The Becker persona matched faint trembles running through the ship to the gyrating traces.

The others didn't seem to notice. No point bringing up the turbulence. "Thirty minutes we'll feel like we're leaning forward," Stone said. He let his arms hang. His thumbs brushed the sides of his knees. "When we round the pole, Trinity's gravitational pull will fall off quickly. In an hour we'll feel like we're walking on Earth."

The ship pushed onward. The rear cameras showed an orange glow at the launch site, obscured by ever-thickening clouds, fading as the rocky surface refroze. Truck headlights winked out of view like distant stars just before dawn. During assembly, Ulrich mentioned in passing the workers would remain on site until the ship returned from Gethsemane.

He glanced at the tablet screens and spoke voice commands. Simulation windows formed, showing the ship's progress as visible from the facility and from Anderson City. Someone in the facility could see the fusion exhaust as a bright spot under the dense cloud deck. From Anderson City, though, the ship would be hidden from view, and should stay that way until the curve of the planet rendered impossible line-of-sight from anywhere on the plateau.

The ship leaned further forward, nearly horizontal. A shake and rumble went through the jump seat into Stone's back and butt. The others noticed too—Caitlyn's eyes widened and Carter muttered more *my gosh*es. The turbulence gauge traces spiked, like an epileptic's EEG.

Laclede's sunken eyes flicked to Stone. "Your flatter trajectory seems less safe." The acceleration and Trinity's gravity pulled on the small pistol hidden inside his zipped-up jacket.

The view from the side cameras showed tendrils of cloud loosing their grip. To left and right, to the distant limbs of the world, the cloud bank glowed yellow and orange. Distant stars glittered.

"No," Stone said. "That turbulence we felt was the ship breaking through the bumpy air between the clouds and the upper atmosphere. Turbulence would have hit on either trajectory." He stared at Laclede's face framed by the launch helmet. The other's sunken eyes held Stone's gaze for a moment, then looked away.

The next twenty-five minutes passed with grimaces and grunts as the ship roared through the empty sky of Trinity's northern hemisphere. Knowing the feeling of teetering on a precipice would ease soon helped, but not much. Deep parts of Stone's mind perceived danger, and all the Becker persona's experience failed to help those parts feel safe—

Stone's gut flopped. Adrenaline flooded him. The combined forces tugging on them shifted back and to the side. The tablet screens showed why. The ship broke out of its tight suborbit of Trinity toward an off-white dot almost a million miles away. Gethsemane.

"The worst is over," Stone said.

The ship accelerated onward. Trinity receded in the rear camera view, and its gravitational pull on the ship faded. Fifty minutes after launch, Stone entered the master release on the launch safety apparatus. He disconnected his helmet from the restraint system, lifted it off his head, ran his hand through his dirty blond hair. "We have about two hours of acceleration at 1 gee, followed by a few minutes of weightlessness as we turn over for the deceleration burn. Then about three more hours at 1 gee before we enter Gethsemane orbit."

He glanced at a digital clock in a corner of the left tablet. Almost 2300. He yawned, but both his own senses and the habits of the Becker persona made clear he wouldn't sleep until they entered orbit. "You should all get some sleep. When you get in your racks, zip yourselves into your bags. They're rigged with sensors to let me know if you don't."

Caitlyn nodded, with the air of a wife who'd heard his speech a hundred times before. Well done.

"What about our weightlessness pills?" Laclede said.

"I'll wake you thirty minutes before we enter orbit. Take your pills then to give them time to kick in."

"Don't we need them during turnover?"

"Not if you do what I say and get some sleep. Any further questions?"

Ulrich stood and stretched. "We'll follow your advice, Mr. Becker." Laclede and Carter took his cue and also rose. Ulrich glanced at Laclede, gestured at the closed, narrow door to the bunks.

Laclede bent forward a few inches from the waist. "After you. And you, Mrs. Becker."

Caitlyn padded in her slippers between Ulrich and Stone. "Try to join me, hon."

"I wish I could," Stone said, "but you know how I get after a launch. It's only five more hours."

"You're right. I know." She slid the nearest suspended tablet out of her way and, with a smile, pecked him on the lips.

After the kiss, he nodded at the tablet and grinned. "Put that back where you found it."

She ruffled his hair. Her laugh tinkled in the narrow space. All the signs of a happily married couple—a vague memory from his late childhood, indian summer in Central Park, one of the last happy moments between his parents before their divorce—

Stone shoved the memory away. Don't shit where you eat, and a man in his line of work shouldn't get married.

Caitlyn moved the tablet back into place. Almost. Time to get back into character. He hammed up a scowl and nudged the tablet a half-inch to the right. She laughed again as she left the control chamber.

Ulrich followed without a word. Next, Laclede. The lanky special agent glanced over his shoulder, gave Carter a pressing look through his sunken eyes. Carter's eyebrows flexed up and he made a minimal nod. A more blatant gesture than he intended, Stone read in the subsequent downturn of his mouth.

"I don't think I could sleep either," Carter said over the deep rumble of the drives. "Mind if I stay?"

Stone shrugged. "Sit down and strap in."

Carter moved back to the copilot's station. He looked like he prevented his gaze from darting through the open doorway to Laclede. Carter sat and strapped in. Over the click of harness buckles from the copilot's station, through the doorway came the rattle of three rack lids rolling down their tracks.

Stone swiped and tapped the right-hand tablet. A personnel safety window filled the screen. He waited until the telltales of three sleeping bags all glowed green. Returned the tablet to its recess flush with the wall.

In a low voice, Stone said, "Your boss doesn't trust Angela or me."

Carter first responded with rapid blinks. "Laclede?" He took a breath. "He doesn't trust anybody."

"His line of work selects for people like that." Stone frowned. "I thought you worked for him, not Ulrich."

"Oh, I do. I'm a civilian employee of the Trinity planetary police. He signs my paycheck, so in that sense I work for him. But in all this—" Carter gestured at the walls of the control chamber as if they sat in the simulator room, and a short elevator ride would take them to Ulrich's fab and the mouth of the fifty-mile tunnel. "—Special Agent Laclede and I both work for Ulrich."

"It took me five seconds to realize Ulrich is a magnet and the rest of us are iron."

—and iron sharpeneth iron bubbled up from the Becker persona.

Quiet. Stone rubbed his eyes. A few decent hours of sleep would put the Becker persona back in its place.

Carter nodded. "He knows how to get things done, plus he knows the will of the Lord."

"I can tell. Hmm. What is the will of the Lord in all this?"

"What do you mean?"

"Why does Ulrich want to find *Lady Lux*?"

Carter's mouth hung open for a moment. "I don't know."

"You aren't curious?"

"I don't need to be," Carter said. "Ulrich trusts in the Lord. I trust in Ulrich." He straightened his shoulders. He reached for the copilot's tablet and swung it into position between him and Stone.

The ship's velocity mounted as the time crept by, breaking 200,000 miles per hour. Still, Gethsemane in the front camera view barely grew against the unchanging dazzle of starscape. The deep rumble of the drives became white noise. It would only be noticed when the drives cut off at turnover.

Carter continued to work on his tablet with few words. Stone checked Carter's actions on the system. He copied logs to a portable drive stashed in his rack and ran sped-up sims of the flight. Stone sloughed out a breath. Even though Laclede didn't trust him and Caitlyn, he should dismiss any thought Stone would crash the ship. Still, if Carter's observation of Stone's piloting put Laclede at ease, Stone would tolerate it.

After all, he and Caitlyn wouldn't betray the colonists until after they found *Lady Lux*.

A countdown timer flashed on the right-hand tablet. "Turnover in ten seconds," Stone said. Carter squeezed shut his eyes and drifted between his jump seat and harness.

The ship yawed about. Dizziness sloshed in Stone's ears. Carter whimpered, then sighed when the drives restarted and the deceleration force pushed him into his seat.

He opened his soft eyes. "Tobias, you must think I'm a wimp."

"Weightlessness is tough your first time. It was for me."

"You're kidding."

Embarrassed memory from the Becker persona—Angela floating through the cabin of their ship with an open baggie, catching globules of his vomit. "I wish."

He tapped on his tablets. "Here's something to make it worthwhile." Stone tapped once again, swiped to send it to Carter. "You're the first person from Trinity since the original colonists to see your world from space."

The front camera feed looked back on their line of travel. Trinity's clouded face glowed in the light of this system's star. Though Trinity looked almost ten times larger than Luna as seen from Stone's apartment, the gas giant Bethany dwarfed Trinity its moon. Orange and yellow bands swirled across the lighted gibbous portion of Bethany's face. In Bethany's crescent of shade writhed an aurora brighter than a thousand Manhattans. Behind the moon and the gas giant shone ten thousand stars.

"My gosh," Carter said. "What a beautiful universe God made for us."

A warm glow filled the Becker persona.

Stone suddenly wanted to go home.

He shoved the urge away. He and Caitlyn would go home after they destroyed or crippled *Lady Lux*. Not a moment sooner.

Riding a pillar of fusion fire, the ship backed toward Gethsemane.

CHAPTER 15

A hologram of a dusty snowball—part of the face Gethsemane turned away from both the gas giant Bethany and any watchers on Trinity—bulged out of the control chamber's wall. The four men crowded along the opposite side of the room. At least in zero gee they could orient in any direction and give themselves the feeling of more space. Stone tucked his bare toes under one of the pilot's tablets and drifted like seaweed in an ocean current. A warm glow filled him. The Becker persona was in its element.

Thanks to the weightlessness pill, Stone's breakfast remained in his stomach.

"Should we wait for Angela?" Carter asked.

Stone glanced at the tablet holding his foot. The telltales on Caitlyn's sleeping bag harness showed green. After taking her weightlessness pill, she'd returned to their rack with a lingering glance. She wanted to speak privately with him as soon as he could. "She won't mind." He craned his neck toward the holo.

In the light of Trinity's sun, Gethsemane's face showed an ugly palette, shades of gray and off-white. A snowball layered with a thousand bruises imparted over eons by small meteor impacts and chemical reactions induced by Bethany's radiation field. Near the north edge of this sector of Gethsemane, a patch of bright white flecked the surface. Freshly melted and refrozen. *Fresh* was relative—the patch could be a million years old.

Or it could be fifty.

No. Stone pointed at a semicircular shadow around half the patch and bright white lines streaking away in all directions. "That's an impact crater," he said. A measuring scale gave the crater's diameter at over three thousand yards. "Not made by *Lady Lux,* unless the pilot committed suicide."

Laclede's long nose drew in a breath. "A good place to hide a ship, then."

Stone's eyebrows arched up. "I don't—"

Then he did understand. Whatever hole in Gethsemane's frozen surface the pilot had melted to hide his ship in would've refrozen as starkly white as the impact crater. On the rest of the dusty surface, the fresh ice would stand out if an ITB scout ship came calling. But inside an obvious impact crater, a casual observer wouldn't look twice. "You're right."

"We can see the patch," Ulrich said, "which means we can transmit to it by radio." His gaze flicked to Stone. "Does any point on Trinity have line-of-sight to our location?"

"No. Try hailing *Lady Lux* whenever you want."

Laclede scowled. "Our orbit will bring us into Trinity LOS, right? If we try to hail *Lady Lux* at the wrong time, we'll emit signals someone on Trinity could pick up."

While giving an exaggerated head shake, Stone said, "I've set the transmitter and the active sensors to not function when we're in Trinity LOS. We cannot transmit sigint to the UN or anyone on Trinity." Stone's eyes suddenly felt sandy. He'd inserted the ship into orbit. He'd set the ship's computers to wake him if Carter tried maneuvering. Or breaking the lock on the transmitter. Time for some sleep.

Laclede's sunken eyes turned to Carter. The latter avoided Laclede's gaze and dipped his chin a few millimeters. They wouldn't take Stone's word regarding the settings on the radio and radar.

Stone turned a shrug into a stretching roll of his shoulders. Maybe they would trust him before he had to kill them.

Ulrich spoke, his voice free of any sign he'd noticed the nonverbals between Laclede and Carter. "We'll start hailing now."

"Are we close enough to pick up infrared emissions?" Laclede asked.

"Yes," Stone said, in unison with Carter. Stone laughed, extended his open hand in Carter's direction. "The detectors are recording as we speak." He yawned. "I need to catch some sleep."

"Of course," Ulrich said. "Our orbit will circle Gethsemane in three hours, yes?"

"A little less—"

"Two hours forty-eight minutes," Carter said.

Ulrich locked his brown-eyed gaze on Stone. "Three passes to see the entire anti-Trinity face of Gethsemane?"

"Yes. Though we might need more passes than that if the pilot doesn't answer our hail." Stone yawned again. "If you'll excuse me?"

Ulrich gave a single nod. Laclede's sunken gaze followed as Stone grabbed a smooth plastic handle and pulled himself out of the control chamber, toward the bunks. More grab bars lined the surfaces of the passageway. He sped along like a monkey from branch to branch. Caught the bar next to the bunk. Rapped on the rolled-down plastic door.

"Come in, hon," Caitlyn said in a sleepy voice.

The door's thin plastic slats rattled as Stone pushed it up into its slot. The rack was seven feet wide and four high and deep. Thick gray padding covered most of the interior surfaces. A white LED strip above the doorway started glowing. Caitlyn floated in the zipped-up sleeping bag in the middle of the space, just her head outside the fabric, and squeezed her closed eyes against the light. Her blond ponytail dangled in the air near a strap connecting the sleeping bag to one of the rack's support hooks.

Stone closed the door and unzipped the bag. Still wearing his trousers and tee-shirt, he crawled in. Warmth from her body enveloped him. The muscles of her upper arm and thighs pressed against his side. Her hair's aroma trickled into his nose.

"Light off," he said, and zipped up the sleeping bag from the inside.

Eyes still closed in dim light passing through the thin plastic door, Caitlyn turned to face him. She cradled her hand around his. Her thumb touched the middle of his palm and three of her fingers rested on the back of his hand. An affectionate gesture to sell the cover story of their marriage? But even if Ulrich and Laclede's workmen hid a camera in the rack, the sleeping bag would block any view—

Her fingers squeezed the back of his hand, released half a second later. Repeated. Three more long squeezes, then short, long, short. Short, short, short....

Stone curled his fingers toward his palm. His middle finger brushed her thumbnail. He pressed and released her thumbnail's polished surface. Long, short, long, long. Short. Short, short, short. *Yes.* He understood Morse code.

She squeezed more dits and dahs on his hand. *Carter stayed awake with you the whole way here?*

Stone shut his eyes and stifled a nod. *Yes.*

What did you find out from him?

L still doesn't trust us. C watched everything I did.

Not news. She bent one leg, straightened the other. *What did C say about Us plan?*

Nothing. C not keeping it secret either. U and L didnt tell him.

Youre certain?

Stone sighed out a breath. *I can see through all his secrets.*

She cocked her head, then extended the gesture to look like she stretched in half-sleep. Her fingers pressed with greater firmness. *Stringing along a gay man?*

How many times on mission have you batted those hazel eyes?

Point made. Her grip eased for a moment. *Whatever Us planning must be big.*

Fits with suicide run at New York.

Yes. But what would he gain?

In Stone's mind's eye, sunlight reflected off the nuclear terrorism memorial. *UN wiped out. Powerful countries fight over Earth and leave colonies alone. U marches resettled on Trinity back through the wormhole at gunpoint. Or kills them. Set up defenses on T side of wormhole to make retaking T too bloody to attempt.*

Or U plans to foment rebellion on other colonies. Or find undiscovered colonies to warn them against UN. Or lead his insiders on another colonizing mission. Or—

Dont play keyhole kop.

Rude.

U motives dont matter. The warpdrive ship is threat to UN by existing. When we find it we destroy it. Head in game?

Caitlyn put painful pressure into the y in *Yes*. She pulled her hand away. "Hon," she said, her voice sleepy-lovey. The switch in her expressed feelings jarred his eyes open. "I can't sleep more." She unzipped her side of the sleeping bag.

"Wake me if you and the others find *Lady Lux*."

Caitlyn shifted toward him. Her breasts, buoyant in zero-gee, pressed through her thin halter against his chest. "Thanks for getting us here." She kissed him, then twisted out of the bag. Her personal effects locker beeped at the tap of her fingers on the keypad. He shut his eyes after a last glimpse of her pulling loose pants up her shapely legs.

A million women as pretty as her back home in Manhattan. Stone closed the sleeping bag under his chin. Sleeves whispered up her arms. She slid over him, then rattled the rack door up and down.

Even without the sound of her breaths, the lingering warmth of her body both relaxed him. Yet something kept him awake. The pleasant comforts of a long marriage. Maybe he was missing something—

Shut up, Becker.

The Becker persona shrank from his awareness, like a fish diving in a murky pond. Yet even after the Becker persona left him alone with his thoughts in the narrow space, he needed long minutes to fall asleep.

Stone rubbed his eyes with one hand as he pulled himself into the control chamber with the other. Caitlyn, Laclede, and Ulrich floated in midair and stared at the Gethsemane holo. All wore thin pants and long-sleeve shirts, yet somehow Ulrich carried off the outfit like a three-piece suit. Harness straps held Carter against the copilot's seat. He scratched his eyebrow and frowned at his screens.

Stone hooked his toes around one of the pilot's tablets. "Nothing yet?"

Carter scrunched his mouth, shook his head.

A digital clock next to the holo showed 1157 Trinity time. "Three passes complete?" Stone asked.

"Not yet." Ulrich's quiet yet firm voice made the situation sound as if all went well.

"About eight more minutes, Mr. Becker," Carter said. "We've seen over a hundred bright spots where the pilot could've hidden *Lady Lux*. No reply to our hails."

Ulrich narrowed his eyes and traversed his head like a tank turret a few degrees toward Carter. Even though zero-gee rendered Ulrich's wild haircut more disheveled than usual and he didn't make eye contact with the technician, Carter swallowed and added, "Yet."

"The pilot is in coldsleep," Ulrich said. "He may have programmed his ship's comm system to require a number of hailing passes, not just one. Another possibility is that his system roused him from coldsleep, but he hasn't awakened yet."

Stone covered a yawn. "I'm not awake yet either."

"Grab a squeezebulb of coffee." Laclede jerked his thumb over his shoulder at the closed door of the galley cabinet.

"Thanks, but I don't drink the stuff."

Laclede's bald head swiveled. His sunken eyes locked on Stone. "What's the scriptural basis for that?"

"Just don't like the taste." He swung his gaze away from the special agent. Gethsemane's dirty, slushy surface reminded him of a Manhattan curbside when spring thawed dregs of snow. "What were we talking about? Oh yeah. Looks like the pilot of *Lady Lux* hasn't woken up yet."

Crinkles formed around Caitlyn's hazel eyes. "Or his coldsleep failed. Either directly or his ship's reactor shut down and all systems failed."

"Fits with the lack of detected infrared emissions," Laclede said.

Ulrich's lips pushed together and out in a frog-faced grimace.

A thought glimmered. Stone bent his knees, unhooked his foot, pushed off. He grabbed an insulated pipe running along the thrust-

ceiling, close enough to rub elbows with Ulrich. "There might be another reason Carter hasn't picked up any infrared emissions. The pilot might have deployed a refrigerant loop. Transfer heat from the reactor into a tank of refrigerant, then periodically let it flow to a radiator mounted on Gethsemane's surface, dump its heat to space, and flow back to the ship."

Ulrich's gaze flicked over the icy moon's features in the holo. "He could reduce the vulnerability window for infrared detection to an hour or two each day." He turned his brown eyes to Stone. "An excellent insight."

Stone shrugged. "Thanks."

A scowl from Laclede was Stone's only other reward. The special agent aimed his sunken gaze over the copilot's tablet.

Carter blinked, muttered, "Bu—bu—but he'd be emitting infrared ten times more intensely if he did that! No one would miss that signal!"

"Against that background—" Stone flicked the back of his hand toward the holo. "—no one would miss a trickle of infrared if he didn't employ a refrigerant loop." He peered at Carter. "Would they?"

The steel put in Carter's spine by Laclede rusted away. "No. I would've picked it up on our first orbits. I promise."

Ulrich drew in a breath like an actor ready to take the stage for a soliloquy. "We need to look for a radiator. Any guesses on size, shape, and materials?"

"Metal or nanotube alloy," Stone said.

"Small enough to be difficult to see from orbit," Caitlyn added. She shrugged. "Beyond that, I don't know. I majored in physics, not thermal engineering."

"Nor did I," Ulrich said, "but we have enough to start. Carter, continue monitoring the infrared detectors for emissions from *Lady Lux*. Mr. and Mrs. Becker, review our visual data from the surface around each melt spot for a radiator. Meanwhile, Special Agent Laclede and I will continue hailing possible sites by radio."

At the pilot's station, Stone tapped commands. A map of Gethsemane's hemisphere hidden from Trinity filled the view. Red circles ringed white flecks of fresh ice.

He gritted his teeth. Hundreds of possible sites dotted the slushy gray surface. Reviewing it all could take hours. Days. Trapped in a living space smaller than his apartment, with the stink of five people's unwashed clothes and incompletely recycled waste growing ever more intense.

Stone rolled his shoulders. Missions like this one paid for his spacious apartment on the Upper East Side. He refocused on the tablet screen. More taps sent video from half the possible sites to Caitlyn, hovering next to the pilot station's other tablet. Which meant half remained for him.

His stomach grumbled. When had he last eaten? Stone warmed a pack of beef and peas filled pies in the galley's microwave. Like the kolaches the locals ate on Freeland, except pungent with an odd mix of spices—Indian? Indonesian?—and each small enough to eat in a single bite.

He returned to the pilot's station, squeezed a beef pie out of the pack and into his mouth, washed it down with warm, mineral-tasting water from a squeezebulb stuck by hook-and-loop fabric to the wall near him, and got to work.

Tiny portions of Gethsemane's surface, about three hundred meters by four hundred, drifted across his screen. His gaze roved the dirty snowy terrain, locked on each darker patch in the mottled gray. A structure of metal and carbon nanotubes? Or a dirtier plot of the icy surface combined with shadows cast by uneven terrain?

There. A straight-edged shadow, fifty yards from a white patch of freshly refrozen surface... and then their orbit moved the camera's vantage point and the straight edge broke into ragged fragments.

He blew out a cheek-puffing breath as jumbled frozen terrain rolled across the screen.

Caitlyn's fingers lightly typed on the touchscreen. Her blond ponytail bobbed in the air. "I'm writing a script to scan for straight and curved lines. The script will help us focus our search on structures that look artificial."

"Assuming the pilot built a radiator with an artificial shape."

"Even if he gave the radiator a natural profile, we'll figure out another way to find *Lady Lux*."

"Radar might work, but it's an active scan yielding sigint...." The Becker persona pushed a smile onto Stone's face. "You always remind me to keep faith."

While Caitlyn typed, he continued scanning video by eye, bright patch by bright patch. Every spot with deeper darkness and straighter lines quickened his pulse. Every spot then dissolved into a fractal clump of ice, bowing his shoulders just a little.

At least this tedious project reminded him never to take a desk jockey's job if his career as a field operative dried up. Better to die in the saddle in an instant than by a thousand cuts of boredom over monotonous years.

"Script's running," Caitlyn said. She glanced at the clock. "1802. I'll heat up some dinner." Her lean legs pushed off the wall, propelling her to the galley.

Stone rubbed his eyes. Smears of Gethsemane's dirty, icy surface filled his vision. Time for a break. "I'll join you."

He pulled himself from grab bar to grab bar across the control chamber wall. Other than Caitlyn, only Carter remained in the control chamber. Where were Ulrich and Laclede? Had Laclede pulled Ulrich out to whisper about getting rid of Stone and Caitlyn once they found *Lady Lux*?

Carter glanced over the top of his tablet. "Find anything?" he asked Stone.

"Not yet. You?"

"The surface is as cold as can be. Should we widen our orbit to observe more with each pass?"

"We're still reviewing video data. If we don't find anything, we'll inform Ulrich we should orbit further from Gethsemane." Stone stopped next to Caitlyn. His drifting leg brushed one of hers in a married couple's casual affection. He asked Carter, "Speaking of Ulrich, where did he go?"

A longing glance at Stone and Caitlyn's legs evaporated from Carter's face. He shrugged. "Maybe the toilet?"

The microwave's door clunked shut. Buttons beeped at Caitlyn's touch.

Behind her, Ulrich pulled himself into the control chamber from the passageway to the sanitary facilities. He spun himself to align with Caitlyn and Stone. "Have you found a radiator?" he asked as he over-rotated. His hands pawed the air in a vain effort to realign his body with theirs.

"No," Stone said.

Caitlyn corrected. "Not yet."

A bing rang out. Stone's eyebrows jutted up. After a glimpse of Caitlyn's wide hazel eyes, his head jerked around to the pilot's station.

"What was that sound?" Ulrich asked. He craned his neck, eyeballed the galley appliances, then the passageways leading away from the control chamber. Hard as it was to believe, some people couldn't triangulate sound worth a damn. Apparently Ulrich was one of them.

"The answer to our prayers," Stone said.

CHAPTER 16

"Everyone secure?" Stone asked. An unnecessary question—the telltales on the tablet showed the green icons of five locked harnesses—but the others all tugged on their straps and nodded.

"All secure. Commencing deorbit burn in…." A countdown timer decremented. "4. 3. 2. 1."

Stone tapped the screen of his right-hand tablet.

The drives roared. For fifteen sweet seconds, thrust pressed them into their seats. The ceiling became a ceiling again. The floor, a floor. A relief after more than half a day in zero gee. The joy Stone hid inside matched that showing on the colonists' faces.

"I'm afraid it won't last long," Stone said. His gaze tracked two-d mockups of their progress along the target trajectory. The red line of their actual flight crept along like a roller coaster car approaching a nine-mile drop. Another display showed the ship's shrinking velocity relative to Gethsemane. The ones digit changed faster than he could make out the numbers. "Free fall in 3. 2. 1."

Another tap. Sudden silence came from the drives far below. Their bodies drifted against the straps.

"You may unbuckle now. Eight minutes of free fall before I'll order you to strap back in."

Despite the authorization, the others kept their harnesses locked. Their choice. Channeling the Becker persona, Stone turned his attention to the controls. He slewed the ship around to point the drives at Gethsemane's frozen surface.

The aft cameras zoomed in on the landing site far below: a bone-white, nearly circular patch of freshly refrozen ice about two hundred yards wide. A dark, straight-edged smudge at 8 o'clock and a hundred-fifty yards from the target site was the radiator detected by Caitlyn's script. The near wall of a fresh crater, dustier than the landing site and with edges more ragged, showed at 11 o'clock, eight hundred yards away.

As their ship fell at 0.01 *gee* toward the surface, the landing site grew larger. The other three edges of the infrared detector came into focus. But shouldn't the buried warpdrive ship's profile be visible by now through its veil of fresh white ice?

"Anyone have visual on *Lady Lux*?" Stone asked.

Laclede studied a tablet tethered to his wrist, floating in the air in front of him. "Negative."

"Me neither," Caitlyn said.

"You worry needlessly." The cold blue glow of a tablet screen bathed Ulrich's face. "The radiator is clearly artificial."

"We don't know that it's a radiator," Stone said. "Carter hasn't picked up any IR emissions. Have you?"

At the far side of the room, Carter shook his head.

Ulrich said, "If our scenario is accurate, infrared emissions would be rare. We might have arrived in orbit sometime after the latest emission. Absence of evidence is not evidence of absence."

Stone's gaze roved the nearly uniform ice covering the landing site. There, was that—? No. "Maybe the pilot jettisoned junk to get searchers looking in the wrong place."

"Have faith, all of you, and use your reason. The lack of exposed or refrozen ice shows he deposited the object gently on the surface. And he would minimize his exposure to hostile eyes." Ulrich's firm brown eyes challenged each of them in turn. "Carter, are we within effective range for the ground-penetrating radar?"

"Yes sir."

"Tobias, I believe we're out of Trinity LOS and can safely use the ground-penetrating radar. Do you confirm?"

"I do," Stone said.

"Carter, begin a radar scan."

The ship continued its fall toward Gethsemane. On Stone's tablet screen, the larger patch of fresh ice near the target site slipped out of view and the target grew larger. Across the control chamber, Carter's fingers thumped the co-pilot's tablet. His breaths grew heavier and confusion filled his soft eyes.

"Status?" Ulrich asked.

"Sixty yards deep. Something's in there...."

"*Lady Lux*," Ulrich intoned.

Carter gulped. "Maybe. I wish I could say yes, I really do, but maybe I don't know how to read the signal. If I'm doing it right, it doesn't return the profile of *Lady Lux*."

"What else could it be?" Ulrich's low voice filled the room. "Tobias?"

Stone shrugged. "I never used a ground-penetrating radar. I don't know how to read the signal any better."

"I'm sorry, but I don't either." Caitlyn's ponytail drifted like a lazy snake. "My college physics major didn't require applied geophysics."

For a moment, Ulrich looked thoughtful. A moment only. Command flowed back into his intense brown eyes and his quietly dominating voice. "The evidence points to *Lady Lux* lying below. Proceed."

More minutes passed. Stone called up a 3d rendering of *Lady Lux* from the ship's database. A cylinder four hundred yards long and fifteen in diameter, crowned with warp rings front and back. A bulge near the rear marked the cooling fins retracted against the body. Despite its size, hundreds of colonists once rode for weeks in cramped quarters wedged around the huge fuel tanks required to power the warping of space.

Not today's problem, he scolded the Becker persona. The pilot likely buried it nose-up. He rotated the image, zoomed out about a hundred scale yards, and took a 2d snapshot of the front warp ring, the main hull, and the six struts holding the two parts together. He flicked the snapshot to a corner of his left-hand tablet.

Now that he knew what to look for, he turned again to the rear camera views of Gethsemane's surface.

An array of fins now showed on the upper surface of the radiator. Moments later, the radiator passed from view. The target site showed ridges and snowy patches in its stark white surface. Not a skating rink —closer to a pond freezing under wind and weather. Still no sign of *Lady Lux* at visible wavelengths or from the ground-penetrating radar.

Stone checked their ship's speed and altitude on his tablets. Though Gethsemane's gravity was feeble, the icy moon had pulled them down for over eight minutes, accelerating them to over a hundred miles per hour toward the surface. Time to cut speed for a hover to melt the ice. "Prepare for deceleration burn."

A glance at the green icons of engaged safety harnesses, then Stone programmed the burn into the drive. At 180 meters altitude, the drives would fire for about five and a half seconds at one *gee* until the speed of their fall reached zero. The drives would then throttle back to about a hundredth of a *gee*, enough to counter Gethsemane's faint gravity and hold station a hundred feet above the center of the patch of bone-white ice. While the ship hovered, the hot exhaust racing out of the drive nozzles would melt the ice to reveal *Lady Lux*.

Though even with the immense heat of their ship's exhaust, they would hover in microgravity for over three hours before enough ice melted.

"Burn in 3. 2. 1."

The comforting roar of the drives thrummed through the ship. A few more seconds of weight pushed them into their seats, then cut off. Carter squeezed shut his eyes and clamped his hand over his mouth.

"Hover engaged," Stone said. "You alright over there?"

Carter pulled his hand clear. His voice warbled. "I'll manage."

"Up your dose to once every twelve hours."

"What about side effects?"

Three hours to melt, an hour to sink into the melted liquid and dock with *Lady Lux*, and a day or two to make contact with the pilot. And then? "We'll be back under thrust before any lasting damage kicks in. Unless Mr. Ulrich plans to stay here a while."

Ulrich's intense brown eyes regarded him. "I don't."

Worth a shot at getting Ulrich to hint at his plans. Stone pressed softkeys on his tablets. "We're going to be in a hundredth of a *gee* indefinitely. You can all unbuckle. I'll throw the rear camera view on the wall."

Laclede and Ulrich unstrapped their harnesses and pushed off the wall, twisting to watch the hologram projected on the wall behind their jump seats. The bone-white patch of ice beneath them filled the view, its edges beyond the cameras' scope. They were close enough to see ridges in the ice and dustings of snow on its surface. A software filter laid a black circle over the bright hot pillar of exhaust. Roiling vapor surrounded the exhaust, melted ice boiling in Gethsemane's negligible atmosphere. The outer edges of the vapor cloud billowed back and forth, revealing and concealing the rippling surface of liquid.

The warpdrive ship still remained hidden deep under the ice.

Stone and the others unhitched themselves and crowded Ulrich and Laclede in the center of the control chamber. The faint tug of microgravity was strong enough to impose up and down on Stone's senses. Like a straphanger on the subway, he reached for one of the exposed pipes overhead. The others oriented their heads toward the ceiling.

"Will our exhaust damage *Lady Lux*?" Carter asked.

"Most warpdrive ships were built to withstand high speed impacts with micrometeorites entering the warp cylinder," Ulrich said. "Tobias and Angela might be able to confirm that."

"Matches what we know," Stone said. Caitlyn nodded.

Stone leaned closer to the colonists. "The view won't change much. You might as well take a break."

Carter and Laclede squared their shoulders toward the exits. Ulrich, though, remained fixed, his brown eyes drinking in the hologram. "There is providence in the fall of a sparrow. So to is there providence in the melting and boiling of water, ammonia, and methane."

The other two colonists returned to their places at Ulrich's sides and stared as the frothing liquid and vapor parted to reveal their prize.

Stone returned to the pilot's station. A two-d version of the hologram played on one display. The other screen showed output from electromagnetic detectors and the ground-penetrating radar. Even though the Becker persona couldn't read details in the radar signal, something large and metallic hid in the ice below them. Presumably the pilot of *Lady Lux* would welcome their efforts to unfreeze his ship.

A clammy feeling stole over Stone's face. What if that wasn't *Lady Lux*?

He shut his eyes and let a breath escape. Ulrich's words came back to him. What else could it be? Another ship striking Gethsemane with enough kinetic energy to melt a patch of ice two hundred yards across wouldn't have left a radiator on the surface nearby. The pilot had placed the radiator near the bone-white patch. He'd placed a large and metallic object in the ice below. If it wasn't *Lady Lux*, what could it—

The Becker persona flooded him with intuitions. Stone struggled to translate into words. A metal-rich meteorite impact could bury a large and metallic object at the bottom of a temporary lake of melted ice, a lake refreezing in a blink of a cosmic eye to form the white patch below them.

—But the radiator near the patch of refrozen ice.

A decoy. *Lady Lux*'s pilot wanted to direct a searcher's attention to the white patch over which they now hovered.

What good would it do? Someone looking for *Lady Lux* would find the meteorite and then search in another spot of refrozen ice somewhere nearby—

Unless they couldn't.

"Everyone. Strap in. Now!"

Carter's head jerked up. His eyebrows arched over wide eyes. Laclede too turned his head, swiveling his narrowed, sunken eyes toward Stone.

Ulrich watched the melting, boiling ices in the hologram. Calmly, he asked, "Why the alarm, Mr. Becker?"

The others froze. Caitlyn inhaled in the sudden quiet.

"The pilot might have set a booby trap," Stone said. "A weapon, maybe a missile launcher, buried in the ice."

A glance by Ulrich to the lower left of the hologram made clear to Stone that Ulrich remembered the radiator. He spoke without turning his head. "We have evidence pointing to this site."

Stone spoke. Heads turned to him like spectators at a tennis match. "The radiator could be a decoy."

"Could. Or it could be in use."

Or it could be both. Stone willed away the Becker persona's chatter. "Okay, it's just a hunch, but if there's even a tiny chance, we need to be ready for evasive maneuvers."

"I follow the logic," Ulrich said. First to Laclede, he said, "Strap in. You too, Carter." As Laclede's hand crinkled over a pipe's insulation to push himself off, Ulrich added to Carter, "And record."

Stone shot a puzzled glance toward Caitlyn. She wrinkled her nose back at him. She hadn't heard Ulrich. Hell, maybe he hadn't heard Ulrich correctly either.

Not the time to figure it out. He pushed off the ceiling for the pilot's station. Strapped himself in. Pulled the tablets out on their telescoping arms.

His hands flew over the touchscreens. He wanted every view he could get. Visible, infrared, radar. Radiation? Back in the Time of Troubles, could a warpdrive ship pilot buy a nuclear warhead from some failed state, India, maybe, or China?

He opened the feed from the radiation detectors. No luck. Backscatter from the ship's exhaust maxed out the screen.

Stone's gaze roved over the data feeds. Other than a widening, deepening pool of steaming ices, no change. Maybe his hunch was a false alarm. Some defect of the Becker persona. But if even the faintest chance the persona guessed right....

He coded an emergency burn into the ship's computers. Five seconds, three gees, angling away from the site. Enough?

Yes. If his reflexes tapped the big green *engage* button in time.

Nerves taut, mouth dry, his gaze darted from window to window. The other people in the room seemed a million miles away. The line segments making up the displays of current time and estimated completion of the melt lost meaning. They could be in cuneiform for all he perceived them. The only clock that mattered was the drumming of his heart. If he could just see the weapon in time.

The melting ice continued to boil off into vacuum. Almost to the top of the buried object. Meteor, weapon, or *Lady Lux*.

He glanced at the nose-on view of *Lady Lux*, fixed the image of the front warp ring and support struts in his mind. Then he cut power to the drives.

Silence permeated the ship. A faint uneasy feeling in his stomach from free fall. Over a minute before their ship would touch the steaming pool in the rear camera view. Even without the blinding jet of their ship's exhaust, bubbling liquid and steaming gases veiled his view.

Not fully. Definitely something in there. An arc of the warp ring? A strut?

Surrounded by slushy ice, the object shifted to a new perspective.

Not the front warp ring not a strut—

"Evasive action!" Stone shouted. He stabbed the green button.

Three gees of acceleration pounded him into the jumpseat. The drives rumbled and the pillar of exhaust shone again. Their ship tilted the rear camera view away from the pool.

A dark metallic streak pierced the billowing steam.

CHAPTER 17

Stone's heart pounded. Dear God, if the pilot programmed a nuke to detonate at a searching ship's hover height—

Quiet Becker—

In one of the side cameras, the missile jetted up into Gethsemane's black sky, faster every moment. The hot yellow glow of its chemical rocket blotted out a handful of stars.

Not detonating. Still accelerating.

Stone cut off their ship's burn. Silence filled the control chamber, broken by a yelp from Carter. Caitlyn's ponytail lifted from her shoulder. They were now in free fall in Gethsemane's microgravity. A quick check. About six minutes until their ship hit the surface.

The missile's chemical rocket sputtered once, then flickered out. Fingers fumbling on the touchscreens, Stone called up a speedfinder. The missile coasted straight up at almost six hundred miles per hour. Fast enough to escape Gethsemane forever.

He exhaled. Six minutes until impact. Plenty of time to correct their ship's trajectory.

Especially because he knew where *Lady Lux* was hidden.

His hands shook, buffetted by adrenaline and relief. Still enough control to program their ship.

Laclede's voice sliced through the control chamber. "What are you doing?"

"Following a lead." Literally, if the Becker persona's hunch proved correct.

"Don't blow smoke at me. How did you know that site was a trap?"

Stone rested his hands over the tablet frames. "I didn't *know* until I saw the top of the buried object. It didn't match what a warpdrive ship would look like. Didn't match a buried meteorite, either. A trap made the most sense—"

"Unless you were trying to get us all killed!"

"You think we're UN agents who want to kill you and Ulrich by committing some elaborate suicide? God help us if you actually believe that. If we were real UN agents, who for some reason gave a damn about the two of you, wouldn't we have killed you already? On Trinity? Where we could escape?" He glared at Laclede until the other lowered his sunken eyes.

Stone looked to Ulrich, bowed his head. "Pardon my foul language."

"Our recent excitement strains us all." Ulrich spoke quietly. "We know you and Angela are on our side." He angled his head to Laclede and added a flicker of heat to his voice. "Special Agent Laclede knows this too."

Another hunch hit Stone. From the real him, from two decades of experience. "But do we know Laclede is on our side?"

The special agent leaned forward against the harness. His fists balled at his sides. "What in the hell are you on about, Becker?"

"Did the files in Mr. Ulrich's grandfather's office say *Lady Lux*'s pilot set a trap? Did you delete that file when you handed him the rest?"

A vein pulsed in Laclede's bald forehead. "You damnable liar." He fumbled at the harness latch. His brows hardened as if they could grind through rock.

"Stop!" Caitlyn said. "Both of you! Honey, think! If Special Agent Laclede wanted Mr. Ulrich dead, wouldn't he have killed him already? On Trinity? Where he could escape?"

Stone showed wide palms to Laclede and Ulrich. "She's right. We're all stressed by our near miss. Sorry."

Laclede opened his fists, let his limbs hang. "Fine." His expression matched the word, except for his sunken eyes.

"We acted with incomplete information," Ulrich said. All eyes turned to him. "Perhaps the pilot didn't tell my grandfather about the booby trap. Or my grandfather forgot to record it. Irrelevant, now. Let us put an end to discord in our house. Tobias, are you programming flight maneuvers?"

"Yes," Stone said.

"To where?"

"The radiator."

"But *Lady Lux* is not hidden in the ice crater we just searched."

Stone nodded. "My best guess is it's hidden in the next one, about half a mile away to the north."

"Explain."

"While we hovered, I guessed the radiator might do double duty—luring searchers into the kill zone and dumping waste heat from the buried ship. I propose we return to the radiator, use the ground penetrating radar to look for coolant lines running from the radiator back to *Lady Lux*, and then follow them."

"I approve," Ulrich said.

At the far end of the control chamber, soft eyes crinkled. "But the other crater looked less fresh," said Carter. "The rim eroded. If the pilot hid *Lady Lux* there the same time he buried the missile here, they should look the same."

"Unless he camouflaged *Lady Lux*'s location to look like an old crater," Stone said. "Another way he guided unwanted searchers to the kill zone." He glanced at the time display. Still four minutes till impact, but no sense waiting any longer. "I'll take us back now."

He entered the maneuvers into the pilot's tablets. A slow fall from a thousand yards over the radiator would give them two minutes to scan with the ground penetrating radar. Assuming Carter could read the radar signature of coolant lines, they would lead to the fresh ice to the north. Then repeat the melting hover. After that... his next action would depend on the situation in *Lady Lux*.

Stone pressed *engage*. The drives rumbled deep in the belly of the ship. He glanced over the pilot's tablets and gave a pleasant smile to the three colonists he'd soon have to kill.

"According to the ground penetrating radar," Carter said, "twin pipes, twenty feet under the ice, run north from the radiator." His fingers tapped the copilot's touchscreen. "Here's raw data plus a constructed image."

A hologram formed in the center of the control chamber. A cutaway of Gethsemane's uppermost twenty yards of icy crust rotated. The radiator turned like a top about to fall over. Two pipes, false-colored in blue, each about a foot in diameter, ran straight down from the radiator, then elbowed horizontally to the north.

"You double-checked your work?" Laclede's sunken eyes scowled at the hologram.

"Yes, of course I did. The raw data fits the profile of coolant pipes going to the next crater."

Laclede lifted his head, as if he wanted to slice the hologram with his nose. "It could be a lure to another kill zone."

"No." Ulrich's brown-eyed stare on the hologram seemed as focused as a laser. "Tobias, take us to the next target site."

"Already programmed in." Stone started the maneuver with a touch of his finger. After the drives pushed his jumpseat against his butt at 1 *gee*, he said, "I'll kill our velocity three miles over the center of crater number two. We'll have five minutes to scan the site while falling. If we get a signal fitting *Lady Lux*'s profile, we'll hover-and-melt again. Any questions?"

Ulrich shook his head. Laclede clamped his lips together and avoided Stone's gaze.

About a minute later, the drives cut off the deceleration burn. They floated against the harnesses as their ship yawed about. After the turn, its drive nozzles aimed at the center of the crater.

"Starting ground penetrating radar scan," said Carter.

Stone cloned the output of the rear cameras to the wall above Ulrich and Laclede's jumpseats. The two colonists unbuckled and pushed themselves into the center of the control chamber. Both hung on pipes like commuters on the subway and turned to the camera view.

This crater held fresh ice, relatively speaking. The ice looked white compared to the billions of years of cosmic dust covering the terrain beyond this crater's uneven rim. On the crater's icefield, though, gray smudges suggested slow erosion had worked for thousands, perhaps millions, of years. A yellow haze covering most of one quadrant suggested the few ultraviolet rays of Trinity's sun had broken down a fraction of a vein of frozen methane.

"How could the pilot have faked the discoloration of volatiles by solar ultraviolet?" Stone wondered aloud.

"*Lady Lux* had an on-board fab," Ulrich said. "A bank of ultraviolet LEDs would have been feasible to construct, deploy, and recycle upon completion."

Laclede angled his head, showing no sign he heard or cared about astrochemistry. His sunken eyes narrowed even further and he leaned forward. "Becker. Zoom in."

"On what?"

Laclede pointed. "That."

A corner of the display, near the edge of the yellow haze, abutting a hump in the ice. A dark area, blacker than the dust strewn across the icy surface. Low to the ground. A thin sliver of shadow showed around eight inches or a foot of elevation. Roughly square. From an overlaid scale he estimated the dimensions as about two yards on a side.

The edges were jagged. In a rush, Stone realized how Caitlyn's script had missed the object, and what the object was. A highly efficient photovoltaic array, capturing almost every visible-spectrum photon received from Trinity's sun. Standard solar cells, affixed together in an irregular shape to look unnatural.

Which meant the hump in the ice…

Stone tapped his touchscreens with instructions to the rear camera. Pan. Zoom.

Aha. A distorted shell of white plastic, three yards high and five wide, rose from one edge of the solar cell array. The shell was concave to solar cell array, and its top end formed a cowl curving away.

"If I bump us toward the crater's far wall," Stone said, "I bet we'll see a bank of ultraviolet LEDs on the other side of that plastic shell."

"With the photovoltaic array providing the power for it." Ulrich's brown eyes drank in the object. "An inventive man, the pilot."

"How did he move it?" Carter asked.

"Sled runners?" said Stone. "In minuscule gravity it should be easy to slide the thing around."

Laclede inhaled sharply. "But why did he leave it on the ice when he finished?"

Silence reigned over the control chamber for a moment. "I have an idea." Stone's voice carried a grim edge.

A glance to orient himself. Would the pilot have pushed the thing from the solar cell side, or the ultraviolet LED side? A man could push the LED bank with his arms without kneeling on the frigid ground.

Stone panned the camera in a straight line away from the white plastic shell. Faint, parallel lines confirmed his guess of sled runners. In microgravity on a sheet of fresh ice, how far could a man shove the LED bank and attached power source?

Forty yards, it turned out. From the Becker persona, gooseflesh stippled the stubble on Stone's cheeks.

"Oh my god," Carter said. "Is that—?"

A squat, wide human shape in a white spacesuit. Face down on the ice. Right arm outstretched. Gloved fingers curled into the ice. Left arm bent at the elbow, hand hidden under the chest. One leg straight, the other bent, like a soldier trying to crawl under barbed wire and tracer fire, and not making it.

"He's dead," said Caitlyn.

"What happened?" Ulrich asked.

Stone locked the camera on the corpse and pulled himself to the center of the chamber. "A heart attack? Someone in poor condition, working harder than usual out here. He gave the array a push, and—" He gasped and clutched his chest with his left hand.

"Can we be sure?" Carter sounded frantic. "Did someone kill him?"

Laclede sniffed a breath out his long nose. "Who? He was alone on Gethsemane—"

Head jutted forward, ponytail bobbing, Caitlyn asked, "We're sure *Lady Lux* was a one-man affair?"

"We are," Ulrich said calmly. "Both my grandfather's recollections of the journey from Earth and the files Special Agent Laclede found agree on that point." Laclede nodded in confirmation.

"No one from Trinity could have come here," Stone said. "And if a UN warship hunted him down, they would have melted *Lady Lux* out of the ice, not left it behind."

Beeps and bloops sounded from the pilot's station. A warning, thirty seconds before their ship would commence its melting hover over the radar signal from *Lady Lux*.

"Strap in, everybody," Stone said. He brought his knees to his chin, set his feet on a pipe, and pushed off for the controls.

"Tobias," said Ulrich. His voice cut through the snick of locking harnesses. "Abort the melting hover. Soft land us as near the pilot as you can."

"Why?" Stone asked.

"There's a tunnel, rather wide, I should think, between *Lady Lux* and the surface. We can save propellant and walk in."

"Good call." Stone tapped and swiped. A short burn to cut their fall, a nudge of the attitude control thrusters, and they'd land eighty yards from the dead pilot. "Though the tunnel entrance might be on the opposite side of the fresh ice zone from here." No time to debate further—the ground was too close. The decel burn vibrated through the ship.

"Possibly," Ulrich said. "Yet we need to land near the pilot anyway."

"Why?"

"To provide him a Christian burial."

CHAPTER 18

"'In my Father's house are many mansions,'" Ulrich said over the low power radio in his suit. "'If it were not so, I would have told you. I go to prepare a place for you.'"

Stone and Caitlyn stood between the grave and a pile of steaming excavated ice, holding gloved hands. Almost like a winter's day in Central Park. Except they stood on a plain of ice, smooth as far as the too-close horizon, free of both the slender branches of leafless black cherry trees and a southwesterly breeze to rustle them. Nanofluid support structures between Stone's skin and the spandex bodysuit made his scrotum and armpits itch. Every second, an electrical signal generator over his belly jolted his diaphragm up or down and electro-mechanical stimulators whirred as they compressed and released his chest, forcing the thinly-oxygenated gas mix from his tanks into his lungs.

And he'd never strolled through Central Park holding a woman's hand.

Ulrich's mirrored faceplate angled down at the frozen corpse. The pilot's left elbow tented a spare sleeping bag laid over his head and torso. A silly, sentimental gesture—his old-fashioned gold plate screened off the ravages that decades of bitter cold had wreaked on the pilot's face. "It is human nature to stand graveside and wonder if the deceased will enter into eternal life. It is human nature, and it is utter foolishness."

Stone squeezed his fingertips against Caitlyn's palm. *We kill them now.*

No, she replied in Morse.

"—did the pilot of *Lady Lux* proclaim Jesus Christ was his Lord and Savior? We have no record either way."

Why not.

She glanced up from the narrow grave. Against a backdrop of a thousand unblinking stars, Carter rocked from side to side. The fanny pack and insulating outer layer over his bodysuit highlighted a roll of belly fat. Laclede stood with a straight back. The standard issue fanny pack at his waist could hold his pistol.

Scout LL first, Caitlyn said. *Colonists still useful.*

"And any record we have would mean nothing. We know the Lord said, in Matthew 7, 'Not every one that saith unto me, Lord, Lord, shall enter into the kingdom of heaven; but he that doeth the will of my Father which is in heaven.'"

Stone communicated to Caitlyn, *For what?*

Was other patch of fresh ice the only booby trap?

"I know what you're thinking," Ulrich said. "He flew our ancestors to Trinity, and he hid his ship here should we need it again. We want to believe this means he did the will of the Father. But who are we to claim we know what lay in this man's heart? Or what the Father willed him to do? We can know neither. We can only be still, and know that God is God, and only His will, not ours, shall come to pass in the end."

Yes. Pilot didnt expect to die out here.

Plan for worst hope for best. She shrugged a quarter of an inch, enough motion to reach him through her gloved hand.

Breaths sounded over the radio channel for a time. "Has anyone more words?" Ulrich asked. Silence responded. "Then we enter this man's body to the ground, and his soul to the will of God."

Stone nodded at Laclede. He turned around, grabbed the handle of a plastic shovel poking up from the heap of ice chunks. Caitlyn flexed her lean legs and hopped over. She kicked ice chunks toward the grave while Stone shoveled in the feeble gravity. On the other side, Laclede did the same. The electrical signal generator and electrical stimulators made him breathe even faster. Stone's thermal outer layer trapped heat that spread the itches to the backs of his knees and the insides of his elbows.

After ten minutes they finished. Liquid puddled where the ice piles had lain. Vapor wafted up from the loose mass filling the grave.

Carter held a cross—white plastic slats carved out of a storage crate and tied together with flexcord—at the head of the grave. With a steel-headed hammer, Ulrich tapped the cross into the frozen terrain.

Work complete, he mag-strapped the hammer to his suit, then put his hands on his hips and stretched backward. He turned his head from side to side. "Now let us think of the living, and find that tunnel entrance." He raised his hand toward his faceplate. A faint yawn sounded in the radio channel. "First thing tomorrow."

Stone woke early. He slipped into trousers and a tee shirt, eased the rack door up and down to let Caitlyn sleep, and loped to the control chamber.

Sitting at the copilot's station, a coffee bulb in one hand, Laclede's sunken eyes scanned a flat projection of the icy terrain under and around their ship's landing jacks. His finger drew a circle on the copilot's touchscreen. A red circle appeared around the new grave, joining a circle around the solar panel and LED sled, and twin lines extending from the solar panel to where the pilot had died.

"Should be footprints and more sled tracks leading back to the tunnel," Laclede said. "I was going to wake Carter to do some visual analysis. If a script can pull sled tracks and footprints out of the images, our job gets easier. But now that you're awake, why don't you write one?"

"I don't have the computer skills," Stone said. "Angela does."

Laclede's thin lips scrunched. "I'll eyeball it until one of them gets out of bed."

"I'll help you look at the photos." Stone hesitated. "Can Carter do what you want?"

"I expect so. He's handled every computer project Ulrich assigned him."

Stone went to the galley, pulled from the fridge a squeeze bulb of water, considered and shoved back into the freezer a bagel with dangling cream cheese injector. "Sounds like he's very useful for your project," he said nonchalantly.

"He is." Laclede's sunken eyes flicked Stone's way. An easy read for Stone. Laclede noted his curiosity about Ulrich's plan and dismissed it.

Stone pulled a bag of apple slices and a tube of peanut butter from the galley. He wouldn't make progress finding out Laclede's plan. Time to sow discord he might be able to reap later. He leaned against the underside of Caitlyn's folded-up jumpseat and in a low voice asked, "You aren't worried about him being compromised?"

Laclede studied the projection. Creases lined his forehead. "Compromised?"

"Exposed? To blackmail…?"

"For his sodomitical urges?" Laclede looked at Stone and arched an eyebrow.

An unexpected response. Stone squeezed peanut butter onto an apple slice. "I didn't know you'd noticed that."

"Showed up in a pastoral counseling report when we cleared him to work on this project. How did you notice in only a few days? Never mind. Forgot where you're from. Half the men of Earth commit abominations with one another, don't they?"

"It's common enough on Earth that a follower of Christ must identify those who engage in perversion, in order to avoid them."

"He's got the urges but has never acted on them, far as we know. I bet he doesn't even admit to himself he's got them." Laclede squinted at the projected display, at a patch of dusty ice. "I leave God to judge what's in his heart. All we care about is that he does good work for our project."

The need to say something jabbed Stone. "Hate the sin, love the sinner."

Laclede nodded. "I'm not going to cast the first stone. Plus, now that we're on Gethsemane, who's going to blackmail him? You?"

"You think he can't be blackmailed because you already know his secret? He doesn't know you know. A pro-UN faction on Trinity—or the UN itself—could have gotten to him before we started down the tunnel to the launch site."

Sunken eyes regarded Stone. Heat from the previous day's argument smoldered around the edges of Laclede's stare. "We know that didn't happen."

Seed of discord sown. No need to pick a fight. "Got it." Stone loosened his shoulders. Angled his head toward the display. "Now let's trace the pilot's tracks back to the tunnel mouth."

They worked for thirty fruitless minutes while the others woke, showered, breakfasted. Stone sat at the pilot's station and played with filters on the image. Ghosts of twin lines left decades prior by the sled's runners suggested themselves. Within a dusty patch, a narrow, fuzzy, thicker line of dirt could have leaked from a bag clipped to the pilot's workbelt.

Her breakfast eaten, Caitlyn yanked a tablet free of a hook-and-loop fabric mount. "Any heat leaking from his boots would have melted or vaporized a little ice. I'll write a script to look for footprints."

"And I'll code one to look for sled tracks." Carter took a bite of the cream cheese-injected bagel, then crossed from the galley to the copilot's station.

Laclede unbuckled his harness. "Becker and I will use our own two eyes." From the center of the command chamber, he studied the splotchy white icefield on the display.

Two hours passed in near silence until excitement bubbled in Carter's voice. "I think I've got it."

"Show us," said Laclede.

Sled tracks appeared as paired red lines on the ice. Most ringed the yellowish area of broken-down frozen methane. "I wrote a script looking for sled tracks as faint depressions in the ice. I figured he left a lot of tracks when he moved the ultraviolet lamps around. When I saw those in the output, I was pretty sure I'd written the script correctly."

One pair of red lines broke away from the rest. They ran east-north-east, in a straight line three hundred yards to the rim of this icy crater. Laclede pointed. "Zoom in."

Carter blinked, nodded. The display jumped close to the crater rim, so close the view grew pixelated. Blocks of white marked the crater, and dark gray, the shadow of the icy rimwall. Twinned red lines aimed for a spot on the rimwall but fell short, sputtering out into red pixels like a cheap United Nations Day sparkler.

"We've got to have a better view than this," Laclede grumbled.

Carter's voice rose in pitch. "This is the highest resolution image we have. Tobias aimed the cameras straight down when we descended."

With a reassuring smile on his face, Stone raised his hand. "Relax. I'll turn one of our ship's side cameras on it." He tapped and swiped. By now he'd spent enough time at the controls that his intended motions, learned by doing, overlapped with false muscle memory of the Becker persona. He found the side camera closest to the spot and maximized the optical zoom.

Off-white ice like the rest of the crater filled the lower half of the projection. The blueish rimwall rose from it. The rimwall cast a narrow, jagged-edged shadow on the icefield.

A straight line at ice level just outside the shadow caught Stone's eye. There, another, joining the first one at a corner and running into the shadow. A white panel lay on the ice.

"You found the tunnel entrance?" came Ulrich's quiet voice from the entryway to the racks.

"We did," Stone said.

Laclede drilled his gaze into Stone, then turned to Ulrich. "Carter wrote a script that found sled tracks. We followed them back to here."

"I still haven't gotten my footprint-recognition script to work," Caitlyn said. "Well done."

Ulrich managed a thin-lipped smile. "Good work, as usual, Carter." Coming from Ulrich, Stone guessed this meant high praise.

A blush bloomed on Carter's cheeks. He lowered his gaze, shook his head. "Thanks, but I'm just trying to do my part."

"You do it well," Ulrich said. "The project thanks you."

"It sure does," said Laclede. He gave Stone another sharp look. Caitlyn, in contrast, arched an eyebrow. Aren't you glad we didn't kill them yet?

Ulrich cleared his throat. "We no longer need stand on the wrong side of the Jordan. It's time to enter the promised land."

CHAPTER 19

A square eight feet on a side, with a shiny, wrinkled strip like a scar running across the middle, the panel lay on the ice. Half in the rimwall's shadow, half in the light of Trinity's sun.

Stone bent forward, slipped his fingers between the panel and the ice. Despite the thermal outer layer over his skinsuit, fangs of cold clamped on his fingers. He hissed out a breath through clenched teeth and heaved.

The panel flipped up against the rimwall. A square eight feet on a side, the panel was taller than the rimwall. The panel pivoted on the crater's edge. The bottom of the panel kicked out toward them.

"Watch out!" Laclede said over the radio.

The others scrambled back. Too late—the panel spun end over end, then soundlessly slammed onto the dirty snow twenty yards from the crater. The panel's impact sent a faint vibration through Stone's boots.

"Sorry," he said. He wedged his hands into his armpits. "Coldest thing I ever touched."

"You're stronger than you look," said Carter.

Ulrich pointed at where the panel had lain. "Look."

A circular hole, six feet across, its rim chipped in one quadrant by hand prints. The panel's edges left faint lines around the hole.

"Wait," Carter said. "How did he get an eight-foot panel out a six-foot hole?"

"In two halves." Ulrich's tone made it sound obvious. "He melted the edges with a portable torch, abutted them, and they congealed into one piece."

"Oh. Of course. Why didn't I see that?"

Pointless chatter. Stone peered over the edge. The hole ran at a slant away from the crater's rim.

He flicked his headlamp's switch. Got on hands and knees—cold instantly seeped through his thermal outer layer and the skinsuit—and looked upside-down into the hole.

A round tunnel slanted down at a constant angle as far as the headlamp illuminated. Bootprints and drag marks scuffed the bottom.

He pulled a rangefinder from his fanny pack. Aimed into the center of the hole's darkness. The heads-up display in his visor glowed with a value, 164.14 m.

The Becker persona urged him to carefully return to his feet. No value in toppling onto his back like a helpless turtle. "Looks like it runs straight at *Lady Lux*."

"Looks?" Laclede asked. His voice shook a little.

"The distance matches what we know, but I can't see the bottom to confirm."

Ulrich stood with his back to the crater's edge. His faceplate aimed straight down the tunnel. "We all need to enter the ship. We start now."

"With respect," Stone said, "we know he left booby traps. One of us should scout the tunnel first."

A faint flex of Ulrich's fingers passed in a moment. "Well said, Tobias. Who will go? Special Agent Laclede?"

"I, ah—" Ragged breaths over the radio. Laclede's helmeted head jittered, though his faceplate showed he stared all the time at the narrow tunnel. "—Tobias got us away from the missile in the other crater. He knows how the pilot's mind works,,,,,"

Stone filed Laclede's fear of tight spaces. "He's right. I'll go."

Laclede sighed over the radio channel, then stiffened his back. Trying to hide his relief.

"I'm carrying five hundred feet of rope," Caitlyn said. She unzipped her fanny pack, hooked two fingers through a coil of bright yellow flexible alloy. Hook-and-loop fabric held a steel carabiner snug along the outside of the coil. With her other hand she pulled a second carabiner from the inner side of the coil. "I'll hook one end to my chest clip—"

"No." Laclede puffed out his upper body. The motion lifted the clip dangling from the breathing assist pack on his chest. "Hook it to me. I'm stronger."

Stone nodded at Caitlyn. Let the colonist save face.

"Okay." She took one loping step, landed in front of Laclede. She hooked the second carabiner to Laclede's chest clip, then handed him the coil. "I'll hook the other end to Tobias' back."

She unrolled ten feet of slack from the outside of the coil as she hopped over the hole to Stone. He turned the clip on his back-mounted air recycler to her. Felt the snick of the coil's outer carabiner, the tug of her hand on the rope. "Ready," she said.

"You know rope signals?" Stone asked Laclede.

"No. Why do we need them? We'll be in radio contact."

"Unless one of our radios fails."

Laclede responded with a shrugging bow.

Stone gave a quick summary of rope signals, adapted from scuba divers to meet the needs of spacewalkers. Amazing what knowledge Jürgen's team in cover stories could compress into a speedlearning file.

Laclede quoted back what different numbers of tugs meant. Stone nodded, satisfied. "Let's do this."

He stood with his heels against the rim of the hole, his head facing the middle of the crater. A short backward hop. He turned on his helmet's exterior video camera during the five seconds it took to land on the tunnel's bottom.

His helmet lamp's glow vanished in the darkness fifteen yards ahead. Stone swallowed dryly, then tugged three times. "Going down."

Three tugs back. "You're going down," Laclede said.

Resisting the urge to stoop, Stone turned his body and sidestepped down the tunnel. Even with the low gravity, if he walked straight down he risked a tumble. Tangled up in rope at best. Trying to inhale thin, low pressure air with a damaged breath assist pack at worst.

On the tunnel floor, a pair of scrape marks about four inches wide and a foot apart led the way down. Scuff marks left by moving equipment? No—the uppermost tracks came from bootprints heading to the surface.

Aha. The pilot slid down, skiing on his boots in the minimal gravity.

Of course, the pilot knew where the booby traps lay.

Stone kept trudging sideways.

"How did he get the tunnel so perfectly round?" Carter asked. "Did he vaporize the cuttings? Or did he deploy a tube before the ices around *Lady Lux* refro—?"

"Keep it quiet," Stone said. Sweat trickled into the nanofluid goop in his armpits. "No distractions."

Carter hmphed yet said nothing more.

Stone traced the helmet lamp over every footprint, every gouge left by dragged packs or sled runners. He wanted to believe the pilot left no booby traps. The slide marks continued unbroken. No pits underfoot hidden by a scrim of ice. Unless he'd hidden one lower, thinking an intruder would decide to start sliding as well and would be going too fast to look down at where the pilot jumped—

He took a deep breath, aided by the breath assist hardware mounted on his chest. He would walk and watch. Nothing would get him from the floor.

A buzz over the radio intruded on his thoughts. Constant, low, more felt than heard. "I've got interference on the channel."

"Not interference," Ulrich said. Amusement edged his voice.

"I asked for no distractions."

"Fair enough. We're almost done."

"With what?"

Ulrich and the others didn't answer. At least the colonist spoke truthfully. The buzz dropped off the channel.

Keep moving. Where had his thoughts been? No traps in the floor. But the tunnel walls and ceiling—?

Calm. Think. If the pilot hid a weapon aimed at the tunnel, there'd be a patch of melted and refrozen ice covering the weapon's niche. The weapon would need sensors mounted on the tunnel wall to know when to fire. Even a shotgun with trigger wired to a low power passive infrared sensor would require a control chip drawing a trickle of power, enough to melt a microgram of ice every second for decades. No sign of that.

Unless the pilot buried a weapon and passive infrared sensor twenty yards ahead. Stone wouldn't see melted liquid dribbling down the tunnel. A weapon system could already have him in its sights—

One tug rocked him backward. He shot out a gloved hand to the tunnel ceiling to steady himself. "Tobias, are you okay?" Carter asked.

He pulled his hand away. It throbbed with the intense cold. "I'm good. Just slow going. Can't you see me?"

"No," Caitlyn said. "You're radiating so much heat the tunnel is filling with vapor."

He glanced over his shoulder. Mist obscured figures in sunlight and a sliver of black sky above. Caitlyn and the colonists looked damn far away.

Wait. In Gethsemane's near-vacuum atmosphere, any heat in the tunnel would boil off ices from the walls. Any weapon system buried below would generate enough rising vapor for him to see.

Stone reached around his back and tugged once. "I'm okay." Three more. "Going down."

The tunnel kept its size and shape as he descended. The slide marks from the pilot's descents clung to the floor. Every few seconds, Stone peered ahead to where his headlamp's beam faded out. No change. Just a tunnel through millions of tons of frigid ice. His shoulders stooped more, yet he kept sidestepping down.

His accelerated breath sounded loud in his helmet. Shouldn't he be there by now?

He reached to his back, tugged twice. "Stopping to take a range measurement."

"You stopped moving, roger." Laclede tugged twice.

Carter chimed in. "We'll check how far you are from us. Maybe we can get a read on you through the mist."

Stone removed from his fanny pack the rangefinder. The numbers in his visor display jittered with his cold hand and his exertion as he aimed it at chest height down the tunnel. 18.18 m to the bottom, give or take.

A hunch came to him. He swept the rangefinder in a slow circle. When he angled it down, the distance shrank. 17.24 m. As he raised it, the range crept up. 18.71 m, 18.73 m—15.82 m?

What? Assuming *Lady Lux* stood vertical, given the tunnel's angle, shouldn't the range be a little further at the bottom and a little narrower at the top? Yes, the range would shrink where the rangefinder's beam spot went from the ship's vertical wall to the tunnel's slanted roof, but it wouldn't drop ten feet in a few inches.

He played the rangefinder over the tunnel bottom again. The numbers confirmed. The hell?

Then realization from the Becker persona burst into his mind. The tunnel bottomed out and sloped up. Simple. Obvious.

And an obvious kill zone.

He put away the rangefinder. "Looks like the tunnel turns up about sixty feet ahead. Will confirm." He tugged three times on the rope. "Going down."

Three tugs responded. "Stay safe," Caitlyn said.

Stone sidestepped down the tunnel. Soon, his headlamp revealed what he'd already concluded. The tunnel bent upward, toward where *Lady Lux* remained out of sight.

First things first. His mouth tasting like cotton, his gaze darted over the low spot. The slide marks from the pilot's boots followed the tunnel floor upward. No pit waited for him to stumble into. But if the pilot hid a weapon system in the ceiling on the other side of the curve, he wouldn't see it until too late.

Don't forget the waste heat from the weapon system would melt ice—

—Unless the pilot dug a vent. We wouldn't have noticed a vent outlet looking like a tiny crack—

Stone shut his eyes, blew out a breath. Give him a live enemy to outthink any day.

The tunnel's downslope leveled off. He stopped six inches from the curve's apex. Peered up past the low spot above him. Mist from his boots writhed upward, over a ceiling of ice as uniform as the last five hundred feet.

He grimaced at the plain surface. Easy assumptions were a good way to end up dead.

So too was staying in a spacesuit until the batteries powering the air cycler ran out.

Stone crouched. He eyed a spot ten feet up the slope leading to the ship. Jumped.

Something yanked him backward. His arms and legs flailed. His back crashed onto the tunnel's icy floor, digging the battery pack and air cycler against him, bending him at the waist. Cold coated his butt and the backs of his thighs.

A tug came from above. "What happened down there?" Laclede sounded shaken.

"I tried jumping through a potential kill zone," Stone said. "I didn't realize I was at the end of the rope." He tugged once and climbed to his feet. A chill clung to him. "You okay up there?"

"Stumbled. Didn't fall."

"I have to unhook the rope."

Ulrich said, "We understand."

A tight inhalation, then Caitlyn said, "Stay safe, hon."

"I will." Stone reached behind his back. The carabiner's catch flexed under his gloved fingers, then slipped back into his position. He felt the ping through his pack. Tried again. The catch stayed open and the carabiner came free.

He turned around to look at his hand holding the carabiner. "I'm unhooked. Setting down my end." His fingers opened. The carabiner drifted down in Gethsemane's weak gravity toward the tunnel floor.

Stone turned back to the low spot in the tunnel. Cautiously, he stepped into the bootprints he made a few seconds before. At the last pair of prints, he paused, stomach uneasy.

Your arms and legs went far enough forward to trigger any motion-activated weapons.

Probably.

Stone crouched again and jumped.

He landed on the pilot's slide marks. They continued about a dozen feet upslope, most of the way to a gray slab gauzed by misty tendrils.

Willing himself to remain watchful, he walked straight up the slide marks. Where they petered out, he switched to walking on the trampled mass of the pilot's footprints.

The slab wasn't gray under his headlamp's full intensity. The bright white of diamondoid alloy tossed bright reflections at him. He laid one hand flat on the slab and knocked on the slab with the knuckles of his other. The slab's rigid surface vibrated. *Hollow,* came a thought from the Becker persona.

Stone took his hands from the slab. His fingers ran over a tight seam in the slab and stopped at a control pad. Despite the thick gloves, he felt the linear gaps between columns of number keys and color-coded buttons. He knew before the Becker persona confirmed that the pad was an airlock's external control.

He heard his grin in his voice. "We found her. It's *Lady Lux.*"

Cheers from Caitlyn and Carter filled the radio. They cut off as Ulrich spoke. "The Lord has blessed us. Let us now dedicate ourselves to the roles he has called us to fulfill."

"Amen," Stone said. His grin remained. In a few hours, he and Caitlyn would permanently disable *Lady Lux*... and Laclede, Carter, and Ulrich would be dead.

CHAPTER 20

The others joined Stone a minute later. As they descended, the light scattered by their helmet lamps didn't look right. He found out why when two figures in close single file—Ulrich and Caitlyn from their body shapes and postures—came into view. They slid on their knees? No. They rode on a thick sheet of a flexible material, about four feet wide and eight long—

Half the plastic panel covering the tunnel mouth.

Ulrich and Caitlyn reached the upslope. He pressed the front of the improvised sled downward, shaving and flinging ice into the airless space. She dug her toes into the icy floor to help Gethsemane's gravity slow them. They scraped to a stop five feet away from Stone and hopped off the sled.

As she lifted the plastic, she said, "I sawed the panel into two pieces with a rotary cutter." She patted her fanny pack. "The plastic was flexible enough to make an adequate sled. A much faster way down than walking."

"I do the work and you have the fun?" he asked, mock-scolding.

"Isn't that what husbands are for?" She laughed. She stomped her feet, presumably feeling the cold.

Below them, scattered light resolved into Carter and Laclede's headlamps. Carter slewed the second sled to scrape ice off the floor and wall with the sled's long side. Laclede grunted over the radio and pressed his shins and the tops of his feet against the ice.

Carter dismounted first, shaking his head. "We have Earth-made videos set at Christmastime with children sledding. I always dreamed it would be fun to do that. Giving yourself over to gravity's big strong hands. It must be even more fun on Earth."

"It is," Stone said.

From the back of the sled, Laclede got to his feet. His shoulders hunched and still his helmet nearly brushed the ceiling. He looked up like a cat eying a leashed dog. "Let's get inside the ship already."

"Agreed," said Ulrich. "Carter?"

Carter squeezed between Caitlyn and Ulrich. Stone shifted out of his way. At the control pad, Carter adopted a thoughtful posture for a moment—probably reading data on his visor's HUD—then mashed buttons with stiff gloved fingers. A six-digit code, 521465, then *Open Outer.*

Words scrolled across the two-line display. *Inner door sealed.... Airlock evacuated.... Outer door opening.*

In the bright white slab, the narrow seam widened. The airlock looked like a Japanese coffin hotel room surfaced in corpse-white and stood on end. A single weak LED in the ceiling activated as they crowded in. Ulrich's oniony breath filled Stone's nostrils. The diamondoid inner door jammed against his back, preventing his escape. The three colonists rubbed against Caitlyn's leg, backpack, and breath assist hardware. Stone glowered, but the colonists all seemed good Christian gentlemen, with no intent of copping a feel where spandex clung to her lean curves.

Laclede's breath sounded like it came through gritted teeth. "How did the pilot process our forefathers through this?"

"If I've correctly read the schematics on file," Ulrich said, and his dispassionate voice assured Stone he had, "the passenger airlock lies below us. We're about to enter the command deck and the pilot's quarters. He designed this airlock solely for himself."

The wall held a control pad next to the inner door matching the one outside. Carter tapped the same code, pressed *Open Inner.*

The outer door slid shut behind Laclede. Then, five seconds, ten... Stone's gaze darted. Shouldn't something be happening?

He breathed deeply. Something was. Something other than tight spandex and nanofluid pouches resisted the expansion of his chest.

"Where's the air?" Laclede said over the radio. An echo of the special agent's voice reached through Stone's helmet to his ears. So too did a hiss from hidden vents.

"The display says 12 psi," Carter said. "Pressurization sufficient. The door's opening!"

A vertical sliver of darkness appeared next to Carter. Air rushed in, buffeting them for a moment. The dark sliver widened. Dark relative to the airlock—dim lights glowed in the distance.

The airlock's inner door opened. Sighs sounded over the common channel. Everyone wanted to get out of this tight space. Stone too, but what would Tobias Becker do? He pressed against the sidewall, gestured to the opening. To Ulrich, he said, "Your vision got us here. You should go first."

Ulrich drew in a long breath, then strode forward. Stone and the others trailed him into *Lady Lux*.

Dim lights set low on gray alloy walls revealed a corridor stretching toward the ship's central axis. To their left, a two-door cabinet ran from the floor to the low ceiling. Carter closed the inner door while, augmented by the Becker persona's knowledge, Stone opened the cabinet. Two hooks at eye level, two cubbies above. One cubby held a helmet. A spandex suit hung like stripped-off pantyhose from the hook below. A breath assist harness and an air cycler backpack rested on the cabinet's bottom.

Backups for the helmet, suit, and equipment buried with the dead pilot.

The inner door sealed, emphasized by a cheerful ping from the inner control pad. Carter's voice wheedled. "Can we take off our helmets now?"

"The pilot wouldn't have contaminated the air every time he went out," Laclede said. "What do you say, Becker?"

"I agree, but we still need to check air gases. The recyclers could have malfunctioned over decades."

Ulrich slid from his pack a flat, black plastic object, about half the size of the control tablets on their ship. He thumbed a slider, opening a vent in the object and whirring an intake fan. A display on the object showed a pulsing circle, then a checkmark on a green field. "Enough oxygen," he said. "Carbon dioxide well below tolerances. Carbon monoxide and other toxic gases negligible. Special Agent Laclede, I know you're ready to get out of your suit."

"I don't know how spacers can stand these things." Laclede undogged the four flanges spaced around his neck ring, then wriggled the helmet off. Sweat sheened on his forehead. He drew a long breath, flaring the nostrils of his sharp nose. His eyes crinkled. "Musty but breathable."

Ulrich and Carter did the same. Stone undid Caitlyn's helmet and she returned the favor. Musty, yes, like some rickety house after a decade of rain.

"Stow your helmets in the cabinet," Stone said. "I recommend we remain in our suits."

Laclede scowled. "Why would we need to quickly escape?"

"You've heard the one about old spacers and bold spacers?"

"Night cometh," Ulrich said. His voice stifled Stone's urge to bicker. "Forward."

They traveled the corridor. Ceiling panels glowed a warm white as they passed under them. The power reactor still worked. On their right, a ladder ran sideways on the wall, for times when the ship spun for synthetic gravity when not under thrust. The corridor ended at an open doorway into a chamber about ten feet on a side.

They crowded around the doorway. Displays and control panels surrounded a chair floor-mounted on an articulated pneumatic arm. In front of the chair, fourteen sliders and a trackball provided a manual backup to the flight computers. On the far wall, a gap in the displays gave access to a door, now closed. A few standby lights glowed amid the knobs and dials on the panels.

Antiquated, but thanks to the Becker persona, Stone recognized every surface, every button, every dial. "The control room."

"The schematics have proven accurate so far," Ulrich said. "The pilot's private chambers lie through the far door. Back the way we came are accessways to the fore and aft warp rings, the fusion drives, and the fuel tanks."

Stone said, "Sounds like you want us to check those out."

"We must know as soon as possible if *Lady Lux* is still capable of warp flight, and if not, what must be done to repair it."

Caitlyn looked pained. "If the pilot vented the exotic matter from the warp rings, we can't do anything. The UN controls all the exotic matter in the settled galaxy."

"Why would he do such a thing? Without exotic matter, his ship is worthless. And your former employers would kill him anyway." Ulrich fixed his brown-eyed stare on her. "Check the status of the warp rings. Tobias, do the same with the fusion drives."

"We can start here." Stone waved his hand at the control room. "But we'll need to look at the rings and the drives with our own eyes too. You said you had schematics? Would you send them to our tablets?"

"Of course." Ulrich turned to Carter. "Check the power reactor, the life support system, and the on-board fab, then assist Tobias and Angela."

"Whatever h—they want."

"I expect no less." His brown eyes took in everyone crammed at the end of the corridor. "Your assignments are clear? Proceed."

Left alone in the control room, Stone held the control stick on arm of the pilot's chair to move it as far out of their way as he could. He and Caitlyn got to work, running pre-flight checks on the warp rings and the fusion drives. Though archaic and laid out according to the pilot's idiosyncrasies, the fusion drive control systems still meshed with the knowledge of the Becker persona and Stone's two days of experience flying from Trinity to the crater floor above. Caitlyn, though...

"I understand the theory, and what I saw you do in our flights around Sol System—"

"The colonists are out of earshot," he said softly. "And they didn't leave any spy devices before they left."

Her large hazel eyes flashed toward the corridor, then her gaze returned to Stone. "If I can figure out the controls, I can rig the warp rings to dump their exotic matter."

"Wait. Are you sure? Two gamma ray bursts will melt this crater in an instant—"

"This crater? Gethsemane would look like a kid took a bite of a chocolate snow cone. We'll change this moon's orbit."

Stone shrugged, then his mouth scrunched up. "We'll destroy the other ship."

"If this one can fly on its fusion drives, we won't need it. Can *Lady Lux* land near the wormhole mouth on Trinity?"

"Yes, but what then? We drive through the wormhole and leave *Lady Lux* for the colonists?" Intuition answered him before Caitlyn could. "If we dump the exotic matter, it doesn't matter."

"It's a plan?"

With narrowed eyes, Stone watched screens of green text scroll up one of the displays. The diagnostics so far looked good… assuming the sensors in the drive nozzles and fuel tanks gave accurate data to the software in this room. "Let's make sure the drives work first."

She laughed at that, drew in a breath. She squinted and sniffed. "Does the air smell fresher?"

A couple of sniffs. "It does."

"Carter must have fixed—" Caitlyn's eyebrows jerked up. She touched her index finger to her lips.

From the corridor came the sound of a footstep. Carter pushed his hands out and stopped in the doorway. "You need any help?"

"I don't," Stone said.

"You're sure?"

Was that disappointment in Carter's voice? "The controls are a little different, but my side of things is the same as I've been doing for years. Thanks anyway."

"Okay. Angela?"

"My husband isn't very gracious, is he? I would love your help. First, I need to figure out whether the warp rings still contain exotic matter."

Carter entered the ring of controls. He brushed past Stone on his way to Caitlyn's side. "Is this the warp ring main control system?"

"I think so...."

Soon, Stone finished his remote checks of the fusion drives, then squeezed between Carter and Caitlyn. The Becker persona knew the theory—the warp rings shrank space around the ship, meaning the fusion drives could propel *Lady Lux* at speeds an outside observer would measure as faster-than-light—but had never flown a warpdrive ship. As they ran diagnostics and studied the warp ring controls, he saw how the two systems would mesh.

Caitlyn stretched her arms overhead. "If I'm reading this correctly, the warp rings have full loads of exotic matter."

Stone's mouth hung open. The Becker persona filled him with a glow. "Praise God."

"Yes, but I still need to inspect the rings," she said.

"I need to check out the drives, too."

Carter looked like an eager puppy. "Who needs my help?"

"Me," said Caitlyn. "For Tobias, if he's seen one fusion drive, seen them all."

"Near enough," Stone said. He flourished his arm toward the doorway. "After you."

He followed them out the corridor. They split off before the airlock, starting up a ladderway. He went down with a ping of his soles on each rung.

Caitlyn's voice echoed down as she talked to Carter. "I can tell you got life support tuned up. Is the fab operational too?"

"Yes, it is...."

Their voices faded before Stone reached a hatch labeled *Drive Maintenance.* He swung open the hatch and climbed out of the ladderway into a narrow crawlspace. Hook-and-loop fabric stuck a toolkit to the wall next to his left shoulder. He yanked it free and went forward.

According to the schematics Ulrich had given him, the crawlspace wound between hydrogen tanks, then around the two concentric rings of drive nozzles. The schematics left out some fine detail. Even with the minimal gravity, thick pipe insulation and bulging instruments slowed him and banged his elbows. At least the gauges verified the control room displays. The tanks held twenty times more hydrogen than *Lady Lux* needed to match Trinity's orbital velocity and land without crashing.

He went around the rings, clipped the drive sensor's electrodes onto the data ports of each nozzle. Stifling air coated his forehead with sweat. Droplets trickled off his face and later pocked on the crawlspace floor. On the outer ring of eight, the sensor's display reported every drive nozzle to be in working order. Though more than enough functional drive nozzles to get them to Trinity. Even so, he crawled to the inner ring, sweating and cursing at obstructions all the way there. Non-functional drive nozzles wouldn't be a problem, but malfunctioning ones could rip themselves apart... and maybe even take the ship with them.

Six drives and two hours later, he finished the inner ring. All the drives looked good. Time to get back upstairs.

Time to finalize with Caitlyn when to blow the warp rings, kill their three passengers, and head home.

The meatloaf, potato cakes, and eggplant cubes on the magnetic plates looked like bricks of dogshit, but they smelled almost like the real things. Steam rose in welcoming billows.

Under his untucked short-sleeve shirt fresh from *Lady Lux*'s fab, Stone's stomach grumbled. He'd worked hard enough crawling through the ship's guts to deserve a meal. Even in a cramped break room mounted on gimbals, seated at a steel table bolted to the floor.

How much time had he spent with people he knew he'd have to kill? More than he could count.

"Brothers and sister," Ulrich said, "Let us hold hands and pray."

Stone bowed his head. Under the dining table, he gripped Laclede's hand in his left and took Caitlyn's in his right. To her he squeezed dits and dahs. *Now.*

No, she replied. *L has only handgun on LL.*

Dammit. She was right. Venting the exotic matter might irrevocably sabotage *Lady Lux*, but he had better things to do than die here.

After lights out, she added. *Kill them in their sleep.*

"Heavenly Father," Ulrich intoned, "bless this food to the nourishment of our bodies, that we may better serve Thee—"

Agreed.

"—in Jesus' name."

"Amen," Stone and the others said in unison. He pulled his magnetic fork free of the table's steel. He put on a playful grin. "Carter, are you sure this stuff is edible?"

The colonist looked offended. "It's standard fab code for extrudable food—"

"I'm joking. I trust you. Let me tell you, Angela and I have eaten a lot worse over the years."

Caitlyn laughed like a tinkling bell. "One asteroid settlement was convinced they could profitably export a blue cheese flavored by mutant mold—"

A rancid taste from the Becker persona's synthetic memories flooded Stone's mouth. He grimaced. "Don't remind me, hon." Carter chuckled, and Laclede cracked a grin.

"Our forefathers," Ulrich said, his tone humorless, "ate worse than that, and less than that, during their flight from Earth."

Levity evaporated from around the table, like water under a desert sun.

Ulrich went on. "We toured the passenger cabins while you checked the ship's systems. Empty cubes six feet on a side, each one housing a family or four single adults in sleeping bags for seventy days. Yet none complained. They knew what the Lord called them to do. Just as we know."

He swiveled his gaze to lock on Stone. "Tobias, do we need to melt the ice around us for *Lady Lux* to free herself?"

"No. Provided we keep the acceleration low until we break out, the hull should handle it."

"I surmised as much. After dinner, you and Angela are to prepare a flight plan."

Stone's heart sped up. "Where to?"

"We will launch directly away from Trinity's settled plateau to test the warp rings. Can we reach an observed velocity of 250c?"

Caitlyn gave Ulrich an intent look. "Yes, but I strongly recommend we step up to that speed."

"Of course. Four hours to full speed, four hours to drop back to flattened space? Returning to our departure site on Trinity with as much stealth as possible."

Why the hell did Ulrich want to return to Trinity? Stone kept the thought away from his face and shared a glance with Caitlyn. She nodded. To Ulrich, he said, "We can do that."

"Set the departure time for 0800 tomorrow. A night of rest will benefit us all."

The rest of dinner passed without incident. Stone and Caitlyn took dessert—a slab of spongy cake surrounding an extruded white mix of fabbed sugar and fat—up the ladderway to the control room. They fed flight parameters to the nav computers and pored over the calculated results. Everything checked.

Caitlyn pressed herself against Stone's arm. "While we're here, we should lay in our real course." she murmured.

Stone squinted at a control panel, shook his head. "We don't put anything in the computers that could reveal the plan till after we kill them."

"You think Carter might log in? But how? He's not here."

"You want to bet your life that Ulrich gave us complete schematics and this ship doesn't have a backup control room?"

"Ah. Good call." Caitlyn opened the ship's internal channel. "Angela here. Flight plan complete."

"Well done," replied Ulrich. "Please be ready in the control room at 0730 tomorrow."

"Roger that." Stone yawned. "Do you have a passenger cabin ready for us?"

"No. Take the pilot's private cabin. The two of you have earned it."

Stone rubbed his eyes. They wouldn't get a full night's sleep, but even a couple of hours in a bed would refresh him.

"Understood," said Caitlyn. "Signing off."

The pilot's cabin had an outmoded and bleak look, befitting a dead bachelor's private quarters. In a narrow front room, a galley faced a table for one. Next to a sink covered in an unzipped zero-g shroud, mummified scraps of extruded food huddled on a plate magnetically stuck to the countertop. Around a corner, dirty clothes huddled like massacre victims on the floor. Rumpled cotton sheets and disarrayed, sweat-stained pillows covered an unmade king-sized bed against the right-hand wall. No headboard, just a lumpy, sweat-stained pillow. A greasy spot—oils from the pilot's hair, most likely—smeared on the wall.

Stone's mind flashed to his apartment after his death, with a cleaning crew of Third Worlders carting off his minimal belongings.

He squeezed his eyes and brushed the thought away. "What's your guess on how long they need to fall asleep?"

Caitlyn gave him a flat look, odd coming from her hazel eyes. "Two hours?"

"Head in the game, keyhole kop?"

She scowled, then her face went slack. "I'm tired, just like you. We could use some rest before we act."

"Two hours puts us at…" He checked the polished silicon face of his watch. "…0100." He raised his wrist to his mouth. "Set alarm for 0100. No repeat." He yawned and went around the bed. Unsnapped the fanny pack's clasp and let it drop. He lowered himself onto the side furthest from the door. Dust stirred and slowly settled. He sneezed. Sleeping in the bed of a man dead for decades…

His eyes shut.

A faint tremor through the memory-foam mattress told him Caitlyn sat on the bed's other side. "Dim the lights," she said. The sound of her unzipping her fanny pack failed to open his eyes. A soft thump on the floor next to her side of the bed was the last sound he heard before falling asleep.

CHAPTER 21

A deep rumble. Stone's limbs sank into the bed.

Caitlyn's voice. "The hell?"

Stone jolted upright against a third of a *gee*. Bright light from the LED panel in the ceiling gleamed on the hands of his wristwatch. 1245.

Two shadowy figures in the entryway from the galley. One tall, the other shorter yet projecting even more authority. Stone blinked. Yes, Laclede and Ulrich.

"Dammit, Carter." Laclede lifted his pistol. Fifteen round magazine, by the look of it. The only firearm on *Lady Lux*.

The dark eye of the muzzle aimed at Stone's chest.

Stone's heart pounded. "What the hell is going on?"

Laclede's hand tightened, then eased when Ulrich touched Laclede's shoulder. "Don't blame Carter. I didn't radio him to wait in time." He turned his brown eyes on Stone. "Put your hands up, both of you, and I'll answer Tobias' question. You've earned that right."

A sidelong glance from sunken eyes. "Mr. Ulrich—"

"Are they fellow Christians?"

"Y… yes." Laclede slipped his finger outside the trigger guard. His gaze knifed back to Stone and Caitlyn. "He said hands up."

Stone raised his hands, palms out above the bed.

Clanging and bonging sounds echoed through the hull. What? The backs of his hands had only brushed the wall. Ah. *Lady Lux* was under thrust, ripping itself out of the iced crater.

To hell with that. The colonists had figured them out. No. Ulrich called him Tobias—

To hell with that too. Answers later. Now, fight.

With what? A sparsely furnished room. Dirty clothes on the floor. Their fanny packs—

Did Caitlyn still have the rotary cutter, in the pack next to her side of the bed?

Like Stone, Caitlyn sat against the wall, her hands on her head, palms up, arms crossed at the wrists. A wrinkled sheet covered her to the waist. She stretched out her toes toward a rumpled, sweat-stained pillow lying on the sheet. Her hazel eyes glared. "How could you turn on us? You told us you would give us *Lady Lux* after Tobias piloted your mission for you!"

"It pained me to lie to you," said Ulrich. "I prayed a great deal that there might be another way. But the Lord gave me to understand there was no other way for me to serve his higher purpose."

Stone grunted. "There's a purpose so high you would kill fellow Christians in cold blood?"

"Yes. That purpose came to me the moment Special Agent Laclede told me *Lady Lux* hid under Gethsemane's ice. The UN destroyed Trinity. More, our home cannot be saved. We cannot fight the blue helmets and their auxiliaries among the resettled. We cannot destroy the wormhole without sterilizing our plateau with gamma radiation. We have only one choice."

Caitlyn lifted her chin. Her lips parted. "You want to flee."

"You see it, in part. I will tell you the whole. Seven hundred people, loyal to the true spirit of our colony and our faith, have been chosen. The seven hundred will mobilize during our descent, when we will call our facility at the plateau's edge. By the time we refuel *Lady Lux*, the seven hundred will descend the tunnel and join us on board, with the clothes on their backs, as many fab-cyclable atoms as they can carry, and the certainty that the Lord has called them to settle a New

Trinity, wherever it might be. Hundreds, perhaps even thousands of light-years away from the UN's grasp. We do not know, but we will find it. After *Lady Lux* departs with the UN bureaucrats on Trinity unaware of what we've done."

Stone's butt sank into the mattress. At the doorway, Laclede rocked on his feet. One arm extended, chopping the air for balance. The pistol in the special agent's other hand wavered.

Stone lowered his arms, elbows brushing ribs. His legs tensed to spring across the room—

The muzzle's dark eye stared at Stone. "Don't try it," Laclede said. His voice sounded as steady as his long frame looked in the now-constant 1 *gee* thrust.

Lady Lux had broken free of the ice, and now accelerated away from Gethsemane. To where?

Stone opened his palms wide and raised them. "Carter is flying us?" He packed his voice with disbelief.

"He trained on the simulator in our facility's basement," said Ulrich. "He can feed the relevant data to the nav computers as easily as you. He has also modeled as many of your piloting skills and Angela's warp ring handling skills as he can from the computer systems' logs."

"So where is he?"

Ulrich gave a cold, thin-lipped smile.

Stone's voice rose. "You've got it all planned. Why do you need to kill us?"

"If we let you fly us to our New Trinity, then give you *Lady Lux* to spread the Gospel, what would inevitably happen? The UN would capture you. Your former employers can crack a mind open and pour out the truth, can't they? Thus they would know the location of our New Trinity. We cannot permit that."

"We wouldn't get caught—"

"'The next time you think you're perfect, try walking on water.'"

Caitlyn's voice cracked. "There's another way. We deny our claim to *Lady Lux*. We go with you and build your New Trinity. Tie our destinies to yours."

Ulrich looked as if struck with heartburn. "I would have agreed to that… except you previously tied your destinies to the UN. God does know what's in your hearts, but I do not. I can only act based on what I know."

Stone swallowed. Dying here? Now? Because he underestimated these colonial religious fanatics? A crevasse opened inside him. His will wobbled on the edge.

No. Focus. Take any chance, however long the odds, rather than meekly die.

In Caitlyn's pants pocket, something buzzed.

With a squint, Ulrich looked over his shoulder, back through the galley to the command room. "What's that vibration?"

Laclede glanced sideways. "What?"

The next moments passed faster than Stone could think. Caitlyn's lean legs kicked the pillow toward Laclede's face. She sprang to the floor in the same motion. Stone jackknifed forward and to the side, landing on his belly on the floor.

A scritch from the other side of the room. Caitlyn had their only weapon. Provide a distraction. He scrambled to a crouch. Clamped his hand on his fanny pack. Threw where he remembered Laclede stood.

"Oof!"

A high metallic keening.

A gunshot. Another. Something slapped Stone's left arm.

He ran around the bed. Dove for Laclede's shins like an old-time football player making a tackle. His right shoulder slammed into Laclede's legs as he wrapped his right arm around. His left leg didn't respond for some reason. The metallic keening raced closer.

Another gunshot. The keening sound turned guttural, like a sawmill blade biting a knotty log. Warm liquid spattered Stone's bare arms. Odors flooded Stone's nose, fresh filet mignon and thick soap.

Laclede screamed. Harsh, incomprehensible sounds counterpointed by the thud of his pistol hitting the spongy floor. He toppled backward, Caitlyn on top of him. Blood and fat flecked her face.

With both hands, she wrenched the rotary cutter from Laclede's skull, so hard it almost slipped from her grip. She sagged with her back against the foot of the bed. The blade gave a high keen. She thumbed at the cutter's control switch but her hazel eyes stared at Laclede's twitching legs, glassy eyes, and the slice through his temple and frontal lobe gushing blood flecked with gray matter. Finally, her thumb found the switch and the high keening ended.

Their ragged breaths and the deep rumble of the drives filled the silence. Her stare remained on Laclede's head wound. "Jesus."

Stone got on his knees. "Head in the game," He reached for Laclede's pistol. Blood and brain fat slicked the grip. "You've killed before." He wiped his hand on the right leg of his pants.

"Not like this. Jesus, why does it smell like detergent?"

"Brain is half fat by weight." Stone found a clean spot on his left pants leg, reached across his body, wiped the grip. "Ulrich ran off."

"Wait," Caitlyn said. From the sound of her voice she'd turned her head a little. "Your left arm's bleeding!"

"He shot me." Not the first time. Then a cold sensation washed over him. "Ulrich ran off."

"I'll find the medkit—"

Stone stood. "No time! Suits and helmets on, now!"

"But you got shot—"

He glanced at his upper arm. A jagged hole thick with blood and torn muscle. Unreal, like something seen in video happening to someone else. "This won't kill me. Ulrich telling Carter to seal us off and vent our air will." He stood up and picked his way past Laclede's spattered blood and brain. Gray matter could be slippery as a drunk girl's twat.

In the galley, the footing was clear. "Move!" he shouted, then ran.

Drive status displays cast dancing light on the walls of the empty control room. Stone sprinted through. In the corridor beyond, the hatch to the ladderway closed the last inch. He'd just missed Ulrich. Next problem, forget him for now. Suits and helmets first. In the cabinet near the airlock.

He reached the end of the corridor, laid his pistol down, yanked open the cabinet. Three helmets lay on the bottom, heaped like the skulls of giant insects. He let out a relieved breath. Ulrich hadn't taken the time to sabotage their helmets. But he had run off with two.

The cabinet also held three suits. Three backpacks, all hooked up to chargers. Eight hours of power each.

Two skinsuits and two backpacks were missing as well.

Footsteps pounded his way down the corridor. Caitlyn coming his way. Good. She knew when to listen.

With one hand, Stone tossed her folded suit to her, then nanofluid packs for her crotch, armpits, and under her breasts. He tumbled his suit to the floor. Nanofluid packs spilled over his feet.

One-handed, he squirmed out of his pants and shirt. Standing in his boxers, he reached for the suit. One hand wouldn't be enough. Hold it open with both.

Pain punched his arm. He grunted. Blood oozed from his wound, crawled over his skin. Tiny motions of his arm lanced him with pain. Bullet fragments, bone fragments, who the hell knew. Get the damn suit on.

Nearby, a long zip. "Got mine," she said. "I'll help you."

Through clenched teeth, Stone said, "Yeah." She held his suit's legs while he stepped into the integrated boots. Before he knew it, she stuffed a nanofluid pack next to his scrotum and yanked the zipper up past his navel. He couldn't even muster a joke.

Agony made him groan when she guided his left arm into the sleeve. "Now lift it!"

The groan became a scream. She wedged the nanofluid pack under his suit and into his armpit. He lowered his arm and could breathe again. Sweat trickled into his eyebrow as she zipped him up. The rigid plate of electronics on the front of the suit slapped his chest. The spandex compressed the air cycler lines like skeletal fingers against his back and nape.

"Backpacks," he said.

"Medkit."

"No!" Stone grabbed with his right hand at their backpacks hanging in the cabinet. "Turn around. And hold this." He magnetically locked the air cycler's inlet and outlet ports to the lines inside her suit. A button turned on electromagnets in the backpack that snapped to matching steel buttons sewn into the spandex.

"Your turn," said Caitlyn. Stone turned his back to her. By feel and sound, he knew the instant she finished mounting his backpack.

"Helmets?" she asked.

"Check your suit first." Stone sucked in a deep lungful of air. He flipped open the inverted display on his chest pack. Eight hours of battery.

Somewhere nearby, metal clanged. A chugging sound followed. Stone sniffed out a breath. Hope was not a planning factor.

Her hazel eyes went wide. "Is that—?"

"Grab your helmet! Let's go!"

"Where?"

"The control room!"

His left hand grabbed the pistol. Pain ran all the way down his arm. They ran back up the corridor. Stone's chest heaved, out of sync with the electrodes and compression band trying to regulate his breathing of the thin air. He shoved his helmet on and fumbled with his right hand at the locking flanges. Cool and sweet air from the cycler line flowed over his right ear and cheek...

...and whistled out the incomplete seal between his helmet and his suit's neck ring.

In the control room, a display flashed in bright red letters *Emergency decompression. Prepare for vacuum.* Thanks for the tip. Stone helped Caitlyn lock the flanges on her helmet and she returned the favor. Her breath roared over the low-power radio channel. "Why did we come back here?"

"Later." Deep red splotched his left upper arm, seeping between the spandex and his skin. He aimed his chin at the doorway to the pilot's private quarters. "The medkit's in my fanny pack."

Caitlyn took a step that direction, then stopped with a catch of breath. "Can you bring it back here?"

Inside his helmet, he smirked. "Sure."

Back in the control room, while she injected him with a UV-activated coagulant and held a palm-sized UV lamp over his wound, his gaze stayed on the doorway to the corridor. Not that Ulrich would attack—because he knew Laclede had fallen, he would assume Stone had the only firearm on the ship—and Carter would follow Ulrich's orders. Even so, Stone had underestimated the colonists once. Not again.

Caitlyn injected his left shoulder with a coagulant. When she pulled the needle, vacuum sucked a hickey through the hole in the suit. The same happened when she injected his right arm with ten milliliters of thick red liquid, concentrated hemoglobin-based oxygen carrier.

"That should hold you for a few hours," she said. "But you'll need a real doctor as soon as we get to the UN facilities on Trinity."

"First we have get back to Trinity."

She waved at a display reporting drive status and the ship's acceleration, 10 m/s^2. The set of her shoulders revealed puzzlement. "Aren't we heading that way?"

"If Carter flies us on the full torch burn-and-turn I programmed last night, we'd get there in six hours. But Ulrich knows, even if we got into our suits, once our batteries run out, our air cyclers will foul and we'll suffocate on our own exhaled carbon dioxide. He'll order Carter to stop burning early and coast until the deceleration burn, to make our full run ten or twelve hours."

"Enough time to kill us."

"Exactly."

"So you brought us back here to try overriding Carter's control of life support and the drives."

Stone nodded. "If we can't do it from here, then I'll hunt down the backup control room—"

"*You* will?" She pointed at the tourniquet around his left arm.

"You're better at computer work." He lifted Laclede's pistol from a command console. "I'm better with this."

CHAPTER 22

aitlyn took to the pilot's chair. With the stick, she nudged it closer to a keyboard and monitor. "When I start poking around, they'll know we survived their attempt to vent our air."

"Can't help it. Go."

Her fingers, clad only in airtight spandex, raced over the keys. Text scrolled by on the monitor. Stone rested his right hand on the backrest near her shoulder. "What have you got?"

"Be patient."

"Come on, keyhole kop—"

"You think I'm intentionally going slow? I'll run out of air the same time you will."

Stone clamped his hand on the backrest and shut his eyes. "You're right." His hand stayed clenched. She might be right but he still had to do something. "I'll look for schematics." He squeezed between her chair and a touchscreen. Tapped and swiped. There. Ship plans.

Where the hell was the backup control room?

"I found life support controls!" Caitlyn said. "Let's see, which zone is which? Here we go. We'll have some air soon."

To the deep vibration of the drives through Stone's boots joined a new sound. He glanced at the inverted display on his chest. *External pressure 1.2 psi* and climbing.

"You're sure that's air?"

"77.5% nitrogen, 22.5% oxygen. Close enough."

External pressure 3.0 psi.

"Good work," said Stone. He refocused on the schematics. Nothing labeled backup control. Had the dead pilot renamed it to fool anyone infiltrating his ship? Or omitted it from the schematics?

Stone grinned. Either way, did the pilot remove from the schematics the data and power cables a backup control room would need? He called up a map of cable chases. Start at the drives and track them upward....

He glanced down. *External pressure 2.6 psi.*

"They're on to us."

"What?" Caitlyn said. "Dammit."

The high-power radio channel squelched in his ears. Stone winced as Ulrich spoke. "We see you survived."

Stone tapped Caitlyn's shoulder. Made a cut-throat gesture at his neck.

She nodded, then turned back to the keyboard. "What do you want?"

"For you and Tobias to accept your fates."

"Tobias?" Her voice caught at the end. "He met his fate. But the look on his face when you murdered him, he didn't accept—"

"Who, then, is accessing *Lady Lux*'s schematics from a touchscreen that's out of reach from the current position of the pilot's chair?"

Stone laughed. "Fine. I'm alive. I'd like to stay that way. I think God does, too."

"You became a pawn of the Whore of Babylon when you accepted the UN's offer to become spies. Accept your fates, and perhaps God will forgive you."

"Please," said Carter. "Please. It has to be this way."

Caitlyn's fingers tapped the keyboard. Stone checked the external pressure meter on his suit. 2.8 psi. 2.9. 2.8.

She pounded the keyboard now.

2.7 psi. 2.6. 2.5....

"Carter will battle you for control of the air supply to the main control room as long as is required." Ulrich spoke with flat certainty. "But even if you bested him there, the ship's course is laid in for landing at our launch site on Trinity. My people will be waiting. When we're in line of sight, I'll radio them the situation. You have less than fifteen bullets in Laclede's gun. Against you will be dozens of armed policemen eager to avenge Laclede's death."

Stone moved next to Caitlyn. "If we're going to die, we want to take as many of you with us as we can."

"Our dead may enter martyrdom," said Ulrich. "You will enter Hell."

With his right hand, Stone tapped dits and dahs on Caitlyn's shoulder. *Can you take over life support.*

She lifted her hand across her body, rested her fingers on the back of his hand. Just two layers of spandex between them. She tapped. *Not like this.*

Ulrich's quiet voice filled the radio. "You hear the truth of my words. Your fate is sealed. Your best course would be to unlatch your helmets. As I understand it, vacuum exposure will render you unconscious in ten seconds. You would feel nothing in the remaining minute of your lives."

Then like how.

Need five seconds. Lock C out.

Inside his helmet, Stone smiled. He pulled his hand free of hers, then pointed at the keyboard. After she rested her hands on the home row, he spoke.

"You're right, Ulrich. We don't have any way out of this. Before I die, though, I've got to say something. There's a part of me I've known about my whole life. I've tried praying it away and it hasn't gone away. I haven't talked about it to Angela."

"What?" Caitlyn asked, genuinely confused.

"I haven't admitted it to myself. But if God made it a part of me then why shouldn't I admit it? Especially to Carter, who reminded me again that it's a part of me."

Carter said, "What are you talking about?"

"There's a—it's a—a temptation. An urge. An inclination. I know there are Old Testament verses condemning it—"

His voice sharp, Ulrich said, "Drop off the channel, Carter."

"What? I don't know what Tobias is saying—"

"I don't either," said Caitlyn. "Hon, what's going on?" Her fingers remained on the home row.

"Angela, I'm so sorry," Stone said, "but all our life together I've been living a lie. Carter knows what I mean."

"I do?"

"You've been living the same lie—"

"What?" Panic filled Carter's voice. "You're accusing me of having, having....?"

"He's lying!" Ulrich said. "Drop off!"

"Oh, Carter." Pity colored Stone's voice the pink of a wilting rose. "Laclede knew who you truly were."

"Laclede....?"

"Drop off!"

Stone said, "Ulrich knows it too. You can hear it in his voice."

Carter's anguished welp came over the radio. A tiny needle of shame pricked Stone.

In the corner of his eye, Caitlyn's fingers danced like a pianist's over the keys.

"He's lying!" shouted Ulrich. "Don't listen to him! You're a good Christian with no desire to lie with another man in abomination!"

Another welp sounded. Caitlyn tapped a final key and flourished her hands, thumbs-up.

Stone reached for the radio controls on his chest plate, dropped off the high-power channel. She did the same.

"Locked him out?" he asked over the low-power channel.

"And started air flowing into our part of the ship. I need to make the lockout permanent."

"Carter couldn't. How can you?"

"Angela Becker's persona knows this old operating system. There are tricks to it Carter doesn't know."

"Get on it," he said. "After that, can we pump out their air?"

"I'll see." She typed, then studied text on the monitor. The external pressure gauge on Stone's suit climbed up, 7 psi, 8 psi. The keys clacked the next time she typed. "Our air is secure," she said.

12 psi. 13.

Caitlyn unlatched her helmet, set it on the floor near her feet. The air cycler chugged once more and fell silent. The display's light shone on her cheekbones as her hazel eyes studied more text. "Hmm." She said nothing more while Stone took off his helmet.

"Don't leave me hanging."

"Sorry." She ran her finger down the rows of a plain-text table filling half the monitor. "I have control of life support throughout the ship. Except for one zone." She pointed at an entry near the middle of the table. "I'd wager the backup control room is there."

"Where?"

"Parts of two decks, above us. They've sealed all the emergency hatches in and out of their zone."

"Meaning we can't pump out their air. Fine. We won't need to attack them if you can get control of the drives and the nav computer from here."

Her face showed she thought about his words, then understood his point. "If I can give you control, you'll land us near Anderson City and call on Gray's men or Holbrook's to take custody of the ship. Their presence won't matter."

"Exactly. Make that priority one. Inactivating the warp rings is priority two. Your people can remove the exotic matter after we land?"

"That's above my pay grade," she said. "They can always blow the warp rings, if they decide two gamma ray bursts are acceptable."

They would. Better gamma ray bursts on a colony world than nuclear terrorism on Earth. Stone nudged the back of Caitlyn's shoulder. "First things first."

The clack of keys echoed around the control room while Stone studied maps of cable chases and floor plans of the two decks above. Where the hell could a backup control room fit? The dead pilot couldn't even squeeze a closet between a labeled area and a cable chase. There? No, that was a standby reactor for the front warp ring. Next to the reactor, the reactor's fuel tank abutted the bundled cables.

Four cubic meters of fuel tank. The Becker persona filled the blank space with storage cells, insulation, pumps, piping—

Wait a minute.

Stone worked his way up the schematics scale, then over to the back of the ship. He zoomed in on the rear warp ring and followed cable chases backward.

He smirked. Gotcha.

The rear warp ring lacked a backup generator.

"What have you found?"

Caitlyn turned. "From the sound of your voice, nothing as good as you."

"The backup control room is disguised as a standby reactor and fuel tank." His smirk faded. "You haven't gained control of the drives and nav?"

Her mouth crinkled. "Carter imposed an extra access layer. I'll have to guess a password."

His gaze landed on the sliders and trackball at the front of the control room. "Don't bother. I can fly us by hand." Roll the trackball to adjust attitude, push the sliders to adjust acceleration. Easy, thanks to the Becker persona.

"I checked that." Her tone heralded bad news. "When they activated the backup control room, they locked out our access from here to the flight computers and to the manual overrides."

"Passwords, then. They can be cracked with brute force."

"I'll try. But if his password is long enough and complex enough, we won't be able to crack it in time." She glanced at the drive status display. Still accelerating at about 1 *gee* in the direct burn-and-turn trajectory. "While I couldn't change the flight plan, I could see it. We're on target to land at the launch site."

"In about—" Another display showed 5:02:18 till landing. "Five hours."

She sighed. "I'll do what I can."

Which wouldn't be enough. Laclede's pistol lay on the console, the grips smeared with brown flakes of vacuum-dried blood. Stone's heart pounded like a gigantic gong. Battle coming. Toll the bell one final time for the two colonists hiding in the upper decks.

The corners of Stone's mouth curled up. "And I'll do what I must."

CHAPTER 23

Stone climbed the ladderway one-handed. The spandex glove over his fingers transmitted the feel of every dot of pebbling from the rungs. Between the coagulant and a local anesthetic, his left arm could function… but any movement of his left arm could send the bullet deeper into his shattered bone, or push a bone fragment through the wall of an artery.

He kept climbing. The pistol weighed down his fanny pack. The helmet, clipped to his back, banged against his kidney with each step. He wore his skinsuit out of precaution, like UN peacekeepers draped in chemical warfare gear on the off chance an enemy had nerve gas and the willingness to deploy it. Carter and Ulrich had suits and could vent their decks to vacuum.

Stone drew level with the hatch to the penultimate deck. His breath came heavily and his heart knocked in his neck. Loss of blood. Must be. He wasn't even forty, no way he could be out of shape…. Keep going….

He pushed the lever to open the next hatchway. A puff of air. No other sound. He went out on quiet feet. Turn left down a narrow corridor. A sealed hatch ran from floor to ceiling.

Exactly like the floor plan. The closed lid on the wall must then house the override panel. He pushed in on the magnetic lock and lowered the lid.

Stone craned his neck. His watch showed 0347. Two minutes till turnover. He shut his eyes and visualized the floor plan. Override the sealed hatch. Then right. Propel himself with one-handed grabs or by pushing off with his legs like a swimmer turning at the end of a pool. Kick open the door to the reactor control room, if need be. Two shots to Ulrich's chest, then force Carter at gunpoint to reprogram the nav computer. Forty seconds, tops, more than enough time before *Lady Lux* flipped around and decelerated. He imagined the rising stomach and floating limbs of—

Free fall.

Stone punched the override code into the panel, then gripped the dangling lid and pulled himself close to the wall. The hatch whooshed aside, unexpectedly loud in the absence of the drive's rumble. He flung himself forward. Eyes up, looking for the next handhold—

A white glare spotlighted a figure floating three feet past the corridor leading to the right. Relative to Stone the figure floated upside down. Stone needed a moment to recognize the glassy eyes and pallid face. Carter. His hand clenched around a utility knife stained reddish-brown. A long, jagged line of murky red crossed half his neck.

Stone reached for a handhold on the flat wall to his left. Blobs of half-clotted blood burst on his arm, his chest, his face. His hand slipped along the wall, his upper arm smoldering.

He bumped into drifting legs. Carter's corpse spun forward like a slow-motion gymnast. Stone's fingers found enough grip to stop. Pain erupted as if he'd been shot again. He grunted. Not just in pain. Inside his subconscious, the Becker persona flinched from the spinning corpse. This man wanted to be a good Christian and you drove him to suicide.

Collateral damage. Stone sucked in a breath through gritted teeth. He pulled his knees toward his chest and started his feet toward the wall.

—the glare dimmed—a boot thunked—a sharp exhalation—

Stone twisted around.

Ulrich's fanatical brown eyes looked without seeming to see. He grunted, loud, incoherent. A gleaming knife blade slashed the air.

And sliced through skin and muscle in Stone's upper right arm. Struck bone. Glanced off.

"Awgh!" Spots gyrated in Stone's eyes. His stomach heaved. Floating in free fall, he kept twisting. Ulrich kept going head-first toward the wall.

Ulrich raised his left hand to stop, his right hand to threaten Stone with the blade. He flexed his knees and craned his neck. Locked his gaze on Stone.

His body still twisting, bile jumped up Stone's throat. His hands moved toward the pistol in his fanny pack. Every inch of motion lanced pain up his left arm. Deep red blood pulsed from the slash in his right. The smell of blood crawled into Stone's nose, into deep parts of his mind. His fingers yanked at the fanny pack's hook-and-loop closure. Again. Again.

Ulrich pushed off. Hate blazed in his eyes. The knife's blade glittered in the bright light behind Stone.

Stone's right hand found the pistol. Lifted.

Fired.

Ulrich's arm moved forward. The knife sliced through the air. Stone's unchecked twisting spun his chest and neck toward the blade.

He fired, again, again, convulsive squeezes of the trigger, one-handed, unaimed. Roaring gunshots rang in his ears. His left arm bent, forearm covering his chest. A slash of pain, arm or torso, where, he couldn't tell.

Their bodies collided. Pushed apart. Ulrich's hand pulled on Stone's skinsuit, lost its grip.

More squeezes. More gunshots. The stink of hot brass. Casings tumbled through the air.

In the widening gap between them also tumbled thick, quivering drops of blood.

Gasping, agony spotting his arm, Stone got his left hand on the pistol to steady his shooting hand. Fired. Fired. Click.

Ulrich sailed into the mouth of the hallway. His arms moved feebly to shield the top of his head from the wall. Not in time. His head struck the far wall at a downward angle. His body crumpled at neck and waist. Two dark red splotches spread across Ulrich's shirt. His gaze pierced the floating globules of blood and drilled into Stone.

Stone gulped breaths. His hands tightened on the empty pistol.

The piercing look evaporated from Ulrich's eyes. The blood welling from his chest took on a distinctive stench. The odor of life blood.

Ulrich's last breath rattled in his throat.

Stone's grip on the pistol weakened. He gulped more breaths. Glanced down at the slash across his upper right arm. The slash shed a blood globule with each beat of his heart. His bones turned rubbery, began to melt.

Find a radio.

Where? Oh Christ, where—

The helmet. He gripped it in weak hands. Unhooked it. His arms ached. Dark spots wheeled in his vision.

Chimes sounded, metallic and dire. The hell?

A warning. *Lady Lux* finished her flip. The deceleration burn would begin in seconds.

He swung his feet toward the thrust floor. His fingers slipped into the helmet. He pressed the manual radio button and blood seeped from the gash in his right arm.

"Caitlyn." He barely heard his own voice. "Caitlyn!"

Weight pulled his feet to the floor. Blood droplets rained, puddled. The corpses thumped down, landing in malformed shapes.

"Caitlyn, here. Need you." The dark spots thickened. "Please."

The dark spots merged into total darkness. His legs could only hold him a moment more. Lie down, just for a second, with the dead men....

A bitter stench roused him. He lay on his back on a hard plastic floor. Wide-eyed, his gaze darted around a room barely larger than the airlock. Over touchscreens and a manual piloting station. Stopped on hazel eyes.

"Easy," Caitlyn said. She rested one hand on his chest while the other stuffed the vial of smelling salts into the medkit. "I stopped the bleeding, but we're out of blood substitute. I couldn't top you off. I got you out of hypovolemic shock but not by much."

Her words came to him through a mental fog. "English."

"You're weak, but you'll survive." A dark expression flickered through her eyebrows.

His heart tapped a quick but weak tempo in his neck. Mouth dry, he said, "You couldn't crack Carter's password lock on the flight plan."

She shook her head, rustling her long blond hair. "Can you land us in friendly territory?"

"I will." Stone lifted his head. She put her hand behind his shoulder and helped him sit upright. He put both hands on the floor and tried pushing himself upright… and fractured bone fired pain up and down his left arm. Gasping, sweating, he pushed off with his right hand. Caitlyn aided him with her hands in his armpits.

Two wobbly steps later, he leaned on the piloting station. Drive sliders, attitude control, three screens with external views. Antiquated, but the Becker persona could fly *Lady Lux* from here. His right hand rested next to the drive sliders. He put weight on it and winced. "Got a chair?"

Behind him, Caitlyn pressed a button. An electric motor hummed. A seat's padded edge bumped into the tops of his calves. His knees folded. His butt landed on spongy mesh.

"And a cup of water?"

Plastic crinkled in a cupholder near his right hand.

He caught his breath, swallowed lukewarm water. Focus. Where were they?

The left screen showed a forward view. A yellowed white dot near the center: Gethsemane. In the middle, overlaid with the word *Extrapolated* in monospaced green letters, a ball smothered with puffy white clouds hung in front of an orange-banded giant. Trinity and… Bethany. The rear view. Software filtered out the fiery pillar of the decel burn.

He frowned. Trinity looked too big for this stage of their flight.

The right screen showed an astrogation map. Boxes tagged *Lady Lux*'s flight path with velocity, acceleration, and estimated flight time remaining.

Stone's breaths grew ragged. They were ninety thousand klicks from Trinity. One hour eight minutes of flight time to go.

"I was unconscious two hours?"

"You needed as much recovery time as I could give you."

A shiver racked him. He drew a breath and steadied himself with his right hand on the control panel. "No argument." His gaze traced the flight path on the right-hand screen. "I have time to figure out the flight path we need."

He had an hour. Though his thoughts meandered, after fifty minutes, a double-checked list of attitude adjustments and burns filled the screen on his left. Over the lowlands at fifteen miles higher than the plateau, he'd flatten *Lady Lux*'s pitch and yaw her ten degrees to starboard. Instead of landing in the lowlands under the guns of Laclede's police, *Lady Lux* would decelerate over a desolate region of the plateau. He picked a landing spot twenty miles from Anderson City and fifteen from the wormhole mouth. As soon as they had line-of-sight to Anderson City, he would radio Georgeakis at the field office for backup. Georgeakis' men would secure the ship until Caitlyn could persuade the keyhole kops to send a warpdrive demolition team to render *Lady Lux* incapable of interstellar flight.

The displays showed the ship's velocity at six klicks per second, altitude fifty-one miles above Trinity sea level. The side camera showed Trinity's cloud deck as a featureless blur far below. The extrapolated view through the exhaust plume gave the same view in front of the ship. The plateau remained hidden by Trinity's limb, but not for much longer. A countdown timer showed four minutes till the first burn.

His gaze roved the list once again. He visualized the needed motions of the attitude control trackball and the drive sliders. From the forward camera, he picked a star right and down from center to aim the bow at. He didn't need the Becker persona. Even with a broken arm and short three pints of blood, he could land the ship as if he'd been a pilot for decades.

"When I take manual control," Stone said to Caitlyn, "hail both our field offices."

Standing to his right, she peered down at him. "Got it." She sounded annoyed.

Had he told her already? How much of a fog was he in?

"You also told me we'll call Georgeakis to secure our landing site and ITB to request backup from Earth." Her eyebrows crinkled, her hazel eyes flashed wider. "Are you sure you can land us?"

The timer counted down. Less than ninety seconds. No time to recalculate the attitude adjustments and burns. If he got them wrong, he'd have to rely on the Becker persona's piloting skills to touch down manually.

"No. But we have no other choice."

A nervous laugh and a smile. "You're finally cutting that alpha game crap," she said. "Congratulations. You're making progress."

He smirked and backhanded the air with his right hand. "The man's got to get to work. Strap in and enjoy the ride."

After he buckled himself in the seat restraints, Stone's right hand hovered over the trackball. Thirty seconds. Twenty. Ten. In the extrapolated rear view, a thin dark line—the edge of the plateau—floated on part of the cloud cover.

Now. Stone nudged the trackball. In the forward view, the crosshairs marking the line of thrust crept to the star he'd picked out. His fingers trembled. The crosshairs overshot. He poured his attention into his arm and centered the crosshairs on the star. His left arm had enough strength to reach and rock the *Attitude Lock* switch.

Stone gulped a breath, then slid the master drive controller down. Not far, fifteen centimeters per second squared. Too little to notice through his body. He stared at his target tick mark on the panel until the one on the slider matched. He gritted his teeth as he locked the drives with his left hand.

He sagged back in the chair. Almost six minutes till landing. Five till the next attitude and burn adjustments. The extrapolated rear view showed a wider sliver of the plateau than it had before he'd taken control.

Caitlyn's presence impinged on him. So did her silence. She alternated between staring at a comm screen and rapidly typing commands on a keyboard.

"Why aren't you calling?"

She stared at the screen. "As soon as we closed within four hundred miles of Anderson City, our radio started transmitting."

"What message? Who to?"

"Can't tell whom." Keys clattered under her fingers. "But here's the what."

A voice emerged from a speaker hidden behind a grille near the keyboard. A man's voice, quiet, yet supremely confident.

"Operation Exodus HQ Trinity, this is the recorded voice of Paul Ulrich. Verification code *ad maiorem dei gloriam*. If this message is being transmitted by *Lady Lux*, the ship is within range of HQ Trinity and my vital signs monitor indicates I am dead. Do not grieve me now. *Lady Lux* is in control of UN agents Tobias and Angela Becker. Special Agent Laclede, Carter, and I are all dead at the hands of the Beckers. Implement Plan Judas. By doing so, God will know you are loyal, and grant you a second opportunity to escape the clutches of the Whore of Babylon. God bless you all. Ulrich out."

A pause, then the recording looped. "Operation Exodus HQ Trinity, this is the recorded voice—"

Caitlyn cut off the playback. Her hazel eyes stared at the screen. "I don't like the sound of *Plan Judas*."

"You're the mistress of understatement."

"What could that mean?"

"We'll find out."

She shook out her hands. "I'll hail our field offices. We need rapid backup when we land." A clack of keys, and she said, "Operative Fredriksen to Interstellar Transport Bureau Field Office Trinity, priority code tango-bravo-golf-fife-niner-four, come in ITB Trinity."

Stone gulped water. His voice still sounded weak. "Call Georgeakis first."

"I assume he monitors ITB Trinity, not the other way around." She spoke with a nervous lilt.

Her voice repeated the hail. The timer counted down. Three minutes thirty seconds. One hundred thirty miles to the landing site. The plateau filled half the view from the rear camera with mottled black and dark green. The lights of Anderson City glittered, late in the three-week night.

Stone couldn't see Ulrich and Laclede's base at the plateau's rim. Judging from the dark green smudges of nighttime rain forest, it should be....

"Operative Fredriksen to ITB Trinity. Priority code tango-bravo-golf-fife-niner-four. Come in, ITB Trinity."

Static crackled in the speaker. "ITB Trinity here." A young man's voice, English in a thick South Asian accent. Stone pegged his type. Some UN politician's son, working for ITB at the end of a long chain of back-scratching and favor-banking. "Who the hell are you?"

Caitlyn rolled her eyes. "I repeat, Operative Fredriksen, priority code tango-bravo-golf-fife-niner-four."

Stone's gaze returned to the rear camera view. Ulrich and Laclede's base should be—

A pinprick of light flared from a spot on the plateau's rim. A moment later, another from the same site. A third. A fourth.

The tiny spots of light came closer.

Chill sweat beaded on Stone's forehead.

"Now we know about *Plan Judas*."

CHAPTER 24

Caitlyn leaned forward against her jumpseat straps to look at the rear camera view. Her hazel eyes went wide. "Missiles."

"Looks like it."

"You are on an unidentified ship and carrying missiles? And you give me a priority code that is not in the standard comm—"

A key clacked. "ITB Trinity won't help us in time."

On the screen, exhaust glow ringed tiny dark dots. The missiles, seen nose-on, forty miles away.

"Hang on!"

Stone unlocked the guidance crosshairs and spun them up. Pain lashed his left arm when he unlocked the master drive slider. Slid it up to two *gee*. The added weight of thrust crushed him into the seat. His heart raced. His breath turned fast and shallow. His forearm burned.

If a bone fragment nicked an artery—

The rear camera panned away from the missiles. Stone switched to the side view. The missiles still fired their rockets, but not as brightly. Boost phase over, intending to coast, firing their rocket engines only to stay on target.

Get past the missiles, and they would run out of propellant before they could turn and catch up.

Get past them first.

Fifteen miles away.

"Accelerating harder and juking!"

He pushed the master drive slider to three *gee*. Spun the trackball from side to side.

Caitlyn grunted. Her head moved an inch forward. "How far—"

"Moving your head will give you whiplash. Keep still!"

Twelve miles. Ten.

His arms felt encased in concrete. One more nudge. Over 3.4 *gee*.

Five miles. The four missiles shared the side camera view with dots swimming in his vision.

Fly blind if you have to. Another juke. Another.

Three missiles in the side view.

Another juke.

Two missiles.

Drop acceleration to 3.2 and spin the trackball again—

The side view showed the night-dark plateau. All four missiles had missed. Stone's right hand crept to the view selection switches, flicked to the opposite side camera. The receding missiles rotated. Exhaust glow ringed them, yet still they grew smaller with every moment.

A new flavor of pain throbbed in his left arm. Part of him wanted to cut the acceleration, at least for a few seconds… but a cold feeling in his gut made him switch the camera view back to the plateau.

Four more missiles rose from Laclede and Ulrich's base.

Dammit. How many missiles could Ulrich's ghost launch at them? Slow down to land and they'd be sitting ducks.

His thoughts swam. Something bubbled up. *Lady Lux* had a diameter of fifteen yards.

What did that matter? And why did his left arm hurt more?

"What's the diameter of a wormhole?"

Caitlyn's voice revealed puzzlement. "Forty yards."

"Nothing to it, then."

He spun the trackball, far, far. The plateau came into view. Bright lights of Anderson City. *Lady Lux* flew close enough for the string of lights along the railroad line to resolve against the gray-black and dark green terrain.

A red and yellow glow stole over the screen. Red lights in the panel flashed. Atmospheric friction, heating the front warp ring.

Stone kept the crosshairs on the end of the string. Manually. Too small a target for the attitude lock to help. A glance at the rear view showed eight missiles accelerating faster than human bodies could handle. He bumped the master drive slider up to 3.5 *gee*.

Head still, Caitlyn flicked her gaze at the forward view. "What the hell are you doing?"

"Landing in friendly territory. Before an internal hemorrhage knocks me unconscious."

"Your left arm?"

Chill enveloped him. "It got worse."

"What friendly territory?"

"Not now." His gaze wobbled between the forward view and the side view. The plateau's rim bisected the view below. The second batch of missiles curled up over the cloud banks toward *Lady Lux*.

A third wave launched from Ulrich and Laclede's base. These missiles boosted over the plateau, aimed to cut off *Lady Lux*'s line of flight.

If we can't outrun them—

Stone gritted his teeth and boosted the acceleration another tenth of a *gee*. Outrun them or die.

Individual lights resolved from Anderson City's sprawl. The glow of small towns and bioseeding facilities emerged in the hinterlands. The edges of Stone's vision turned black.

He locked his view on the crosshairs. The railroad line no longer ran at them. Adjust. Lock.

Caitlyn stared at the forward view. "We're going to run the wormhole?"

He stopped himself from nodding. The gesture might knock him unconscious and kill them both. "Yes."

"We're going to shoot a twenty yard gap in a ship fifteen yards in diameter, going at, what's are speed?"

"About eight thousand feet per second." His voice sounded distant in his ears. "Over ten thousand when we arrive." His brow crinkled. "You said forty yards."

"Half the wormhole is buried. At the speed we'll be going, what happens if the ship hits the junction between the wormhole and normal space?"

"We die."

"Jesus, can you do this?"

Two miles above the plateau. Twenty miles from the wormhole. Everyone on Trinity could see them blazing across the sky.

And see the eight missiles chasing them.

Blackness crept closer to the center of his vision. He focused on the crosshairs. His fingertips moved the trackball a millimeter at a time, keeping the crosshairs just above the end of the railroad line. Where was the wormhole? Shouldn't he see it by now?

Not if it was night over the Earth side of the wormhole.

At the bottom edge of his vision, rainforest blurred by. Speed and the yellow-red glow of atmospheric heating smeared the lights along the rail line into a meandering beaded string. Though the engines roared and hull temperature sensors bleated alarms, the only sound he noticed was Caitlyn's sharp inhalation. The sustained high acceleration injured her, or had the missiles caught up?

Stone's fingers feathered the trackball, keeping the crosshairs centered on a target invisibly small. Blackness narrowed his vision even further. The atmospheric friction glow almost smothered the rail line's lights. A barely visible lifeline. Keep the crosshairs on where the wormhole must be—

The glow of atmospheric friction in the front camera flashed red. Stone lifted *Lady Lux*'s nose a fraction. An agonizing moment of even greater weight. A flash of blue.

He spun the trackball hard, pointing the ship's nose straight up.

The rear camera view showed a nighttime rainforest. A line of fire sliced through the trees and across a gently-curving railroad line. The far end of the blaze billowed fifty yards from the narrow black arch of the wormhole's equilibrator ring.

Lady Lux rose. The line of fire shrank. The vast rainforest extended unbroken for miles. The only illumination for the spongy, dark green mass of tree canopies came from a three-quarter moon low in the eastern sky.

Stone's dwindling gaze returned to the wormhole. The equilibrator ring was too thin to see, but the lines of the forest fire and the rail line pointed at.

No missiles came through.

"Oh my god." Caitlyn's voice fluttered. "We made it!"

Stone slid the master drive down to zero. His body drifted against the seat restraints.

Warning appeared on the forward view, overlaid on a view of tropical constellations. *Cannot find target landing site. Cannot compute trajectory to target landing site.* A pause. More words scrolled up. *Warning. Cannot find target landing site. Cannot compute—*

His vision blanked for a moment. His heart raced. His vision returned enough to see Caitlyn's lips move. Then his hearing returned. "What does that mean?"

"Carter's flight plan voided. Autopilot can land us. Pick an empty spot."

"What? Me?"

"I got us through. Can't do more...." He swatted his hand toward the keyboard. "Autopilot. You can do it." A number came to him from somewhere. "Ten minutes before we splat. You...."

Blackness swept over his sight. Silence smothered his hearing.

EPILOGUE

"I have to reprimand you," Gray said.

With a cast on his left arm, Stone sat facing the old man's desk. Outside the window, a handful of puffy clouds flitted across a bright blue sky. The sun threw the slanted shadows of nearby skyscrapers halfway to Brooklyn.

He sipped sparkling water with his right hand. A lazy smirk crossed his mouth. "For what?"

"A fire burned a thousand square miles of the Sarawak rain forest and destroyed a five-mile length of the railroad line straddling the Trinity wormhole. Two hundred million people saw an unidentified spacecraft over Borneo and central Indonesia. An Australian Army battalion training at the outback military base Ms. Fredriksen chose for landing required memory suppression."

"She saved my life by landing there." Vague memories from the edge of consciousness. An operating theater's bright lights. A surgeon giving his robots orders in an Australian accent.

Guarded hazel eyes watching him over a surgical mask.

"To prevent rumors of a partial loss of wormhole equilibrator integrity from spreading worldwide, we had to implement real-time targeted editing of private communications in parts of four countries.

This will cost UNICA over a hundred billion dollars and a hundred favors to other UN agencies, member governments, and NGOs."

Stone squirmed in his seat. "If we'd tried to land *Lady Lux* on Trinity, we would have been destroyed—"

His eyes like discs of granite, Gray peered down his nose at Stone. "Between the two of us, you made the best choice during the approach to Trinity. To the people I must answer to, however, you behaved irresponsibly, and I have to tell them my loose cannon operative has been punished."

"Sure." A smirk crept back into the corners of Stone's mouth.

Gray lifted his whisky glass from his desk. He inhaled thick aromas of moss and sea, then sipped. "After the doctors clear you, you will be removed from the active duty roster for six months."

The smirk vanished. "Six months!?"

The thick bottom of Gray's glass thumped against a leather coaster. "The decision is final."

"Oh, I get it. That's what you told the desk jockeys at UN headquarters. You won't talk to me till the winter but I'll still get assignments from—"

"No. You'll be off active duty."

Stone's left arm throbbed. Gray's words bounced around his mind. More than six months out of action. No. Out of *this* action. He'd remain in Manhattan for the rest of the summer, amid a hundred thousand girls fresh out of college, wearing pleated dresses hemmed four inches above the knee....

"Though you won't listen to my advice," Gray said, "I strongly recommend you forget about seducing foolish young women and instead spend those six months contemplating your future in our line of work."

Stone snapped his gaze onto Gray's face. "You want me to quit?"

"No. You're one of my better operatives. Yet you underestimated your opponents twice in the span of three hours, and nearly died as a result."

"A mistake. I won't make it again."

"You aren't the first man to sit across from me and say that. None of the others who said that lived to retirement age."

"Someone has to be the first."

Gray reached for his whisky. He rested the glass on his palm and cradled his fingers around it like an old dragon clutching a jewel. He swirled the glass. Brown light gyred inside. "Would that you were."

A faint echo of something the Becker persona might say came to Stone. He twisted it with a smirk. "Oh ye of little faith."

ABOUT THE AUTHOR

I'm **Raymund Eich.** I use my Middle American upbringing as a launchpad for journeys to the ends of the Universe.

Growing up in the Midwest prepared me for my academic career, culminating with a Ph.D. in biochemistry from Rice University. It helps me help inventors prosper from their progress in medicine, biotechnology, and green energy.

Above all, it inspires me to write science fiction and fantasy about ordinary people facing extraordinary wonders and horrors, battling enemies both foreign and domestic, and building better lives for themselves, their families, and their societies.

My last name has one syllable and is pronounced "eye-sh." I live in Houston with my family.

Connect with me at **www.raymundeich.com** or follow the QR code below.

Online and brick-and-mortar bookstores around the world list millions of books, with thousands more published every day. I'm glad you discovered this one.

If you'd like to know when I release a new book, instead of leaving it to chance, join my Readers Club. I'll email you from time to time with publishing news, off-beat patents, a short personal update, or a reminder about an older book of mine you might have missed.

Yes, please! I'll go to **www.raymundeich.com/mailing-list** or scan the QR code below.

No thanks. I'll take my chances next time I look for your books.

OTHER BOOKS BY THE AUTHOR

Available wherever books are sold.

Learn more about these titles at our website, **www.cv2books.com,** or follow the QR code below.

STONE CHALMERS

Earth barely survived the 21st Century.

Biotechnological and nuclear terrorism, civil war, famine, and ethnic cleansing killed billions. Thousands fled on warpdrive ships to colonize planets around distant suns.

In the 22nd century, after Earth unified under one world government, it opened wormhole links to the distant colonies, to prevent a repeat of the previous century's chaos on a galactic scale.

Enter operative Stone Chalmers. Spy. Assassin. Instrument maintaining Earth's dominion over all human worlds.

Opposing him are hostile forces on colony worlds… and within the Earth government itself.

When Stone clashes with those forces, Earth—and every human world—will be transformed forever.

Learn more about the Stone Chalmers series at **www.cv2books.com/stone-chalmers**, or follow the QR code below.

The Freeland Vendetta

On the newly rediscovered colony world Freeland, a conspiracy plans a powerful blow against Earth's control of the planet. A blow supported by treacherous forces inside the government of Earth.

The Trinity Deception

From the religious colony world of Trinity come clues of a long-lost prize. The last warpdrive ship outside Earth's control.

The Minerva Conspiracy

Expecting a mission beneath his talents, Stone fights for his life—and soul—against a terrifying conspiracy.

The Terra Betrayal

Schemes and plots from the colonies and the capital converge in the halls of power on Earth itself. Only Stone can fight his way through a web of intrigue and bring freedom to all human worlds.

THE INCEPTI CATACLYSM

The entire galaxy knows about the Incepti Cataclysm. The occupation force from Vela destroyed a planet with nanotechnology. Only a few Inceptis fled the wave of death in time to join their brethren scattered across the Democracy.

Everything the galaxy knows is a lie.

Anara Orden. Daughter of survivors. Recruited by fellow Inceptis to join Democracy intelligence. Though young and good of heart, she kills without qualms. She knows her employers only order her to terminate Velan agents threatening the Democracy.

But when her next target is a fellow Incepti, she questions everything and chooses a new mission. She will share the truth with friend and foe alike.

Yet powerful forces across the galaxy will do whatever it takes to cling to power. Even if millions of innocents must die.

Escape from Conatus (Book One)

When Anara learns the truth, a simple mission becomes a flight for survival.

Revelation in Vela (Book Two)

Instead of a refuge, Anara and her companions end up in the cross-hairs—of two sides.

Victory for Carina (Book Three)

As war comes to the galaxy, only Anara's desperate plan can bring a just and lasting peace.

THE FALSE FLAG WAR

Concordia's mission reflected the best of the human race. Crew and scientists from both of Earth's rival factions, Humanists and Traditionalists, journeyed for years at relativistic speeds to reach Bravo Charlie, a life-bearing planet orbiting Alpha Centauri B, to expand the frontiers of knowledge for all.

Concordia's mission also reflected humanity at its worst. Corrupt bureaucrats and ambitious political leaders in both factions maintained a status quo backed by weapons of mass destruction. The faction commanders on the mission each sought to seize advantages for their side alone.

Then the ship received transmissions. Signs of an ancient, powerful alien presence on the planet below.

Exploration 2127

Sent to explore, **Jaeger** and **McIlroy**, born and raised in a Texas divided by razor wire and minefields. Men torn between the mission's ideals and orders from their respective faction commanders, oily Varanathan and domineering Sandford.

Then Jaeger and McIlroy discover how to bring Earth's factions together... using knowledge given by aliens dead over a million years.

Invasion 2132

Concordia fell silent. Mission control now detects an unknown ship leaving the Alpha Centauri system. Heading to Earth at relativistic speeds. Silent about its purpose. Its crew unknown.

Earth's one chance: Its rival factions must work for mutual defense, against shadowy figures who strive to use the unknown ship for their own faction's gain.

THE CONFEDERATED WORLDS

The purpose of all other combat arms is to put the infantryman in sole possession of the battlefield.

A thousand years from now, while Earth sleeps in virtual reality, three polities—the Confederated Worlds, the Unity, and the Progressive Republic—strive to connect the scattered, terraformed worlds of humankind by artificial wormholes.

When they meet, they clash, in a decades-long struggle of arms that will embroil every human world, in which dedication to duty liberates worlds—and oneself.

Learn more about the Confederated Worlds series at **www.cv2books.com/the-confederated-worlds**, or follow the QR code below.

Take the Shilling

The Confederated Worlds implanted in his brain the skills to make him a
soldier. Tomas Neumann had to learn for himself how to survive interstellar
war.

Operation Iago

The Confederated Worlds lost the war. Can Lt. Tomas Neumann win the peace
against elusive, deceptive foes out to turn the Confederated Worlds against
itself?

A Bodyguard of Lies

Assigned to the halls of power, only Capt. Tomas Neumann can save the
Confederated Worlds from the ultimate treachery.

OTHER NOVELS

The Blank Slate

Neuroscience entrepreneur Clay Shieffer must stop a tyrannical president… because he unwittingly gave the tyrant power over the human mind.

New California

After New California's founder committed suicide, two men vied to rule the colony.

Ashwin George, supported by the colony's elite and the Chinese company dominating half the settled galaxy.

Against him, Desmond Park, nanotechnology engineer, armed with the most formidable weapon of all.

A single idea.

The Reincarnation Run

Skeptical spacejock Landry Krieger knows exactly how to smuggle the "reborn" spiritual leader of an oppressed people past their conquerors... but the boy's priests—and governess—shake up his orderly plans.

Azureseas: Cantrell's War

Ross Cantrell joined the animal control mission on the newly-discovered planet Azureseas to earn the money to start married life together with his girlfriend.

Then Ross discovers the truth about the planet's "animals."

SHORT NOVELS

Love and Death in the City of Bone

He had a month to learn the planet's mysteries—and Juliette's.

His cover story: return to Elard to dismantle his sect's missionary work to the planet's natives.

His true mission: investigate decades-old mysteries of love and death.

His objective: return to Earth with his discovery.

If he can.

A Mighty Fortress

Theodore and his team from the Lutheran Interstellar Terraforming Society would transform a barren, rocky world into a refuge of faith and life.

Or die trying.

Winner and the Poacher

A Portia Oakeshott, Dinosaur Veterinarian Short Novel

As a consultant to law enforcement, Portia confronts stark evidence of a rich young man's crime: the mounted head of a massive herbivorous *Wintonotitan*. A winner.

A dinosaur the company never granted a permit for hunting.

SHORT STORY COLLECTIONS

The First Voyages: The Complete Science Fiction Stories 1998-2012

From 21st century asteroid settlements to World War II Romania, from an Earth dominated by immortal aliens to Christ's empty tomb, a fresh, distinctive voice in science fiction will take you on journeys to the photosphere of the sun, the coding regions of DNA, and the complexities of the human psyche.

Stage Separations: The Complete Science Fiction Stories 2013-2018

In these pages, you can...

...race against time to solve mysteries hidden in a planet's vast desert—and in a woman's heart

...learn the true story of a president's assassination

...journey 14,000 miles to a high-tech fountain of youth

...win or go "home"—to an Earth you've never seen

and explore six other worlds created by a distinctive voice in twenty-first century science fiction.

Orbital Maneuvers: The Complete Science Fiction Stories 2019-2020

In these pages, you can join–

A mission to terraform a lifeless, rocky planet | A private detective uncovering the ultimate crime | A woman called by an ex-boyfriend… who's been dead twenty years | A President breaking his country's highest law | A star athlete discovering the true price of a championship

–and enjoy five more tales, in the latest installment of the Complete Science Fiction Stories of Raymund Eich.

Extravehicular Activities: The Complete Science Fiction Stories 2021-2022

Leave the safety of your space capsule for the dangers of billion-year old alien derelicts, intelligent insects with mysterious motives, espionage in an alternate 1920s Paris, and rogue reconstructed dinosaurs.

These wonders and more await in the fourth volume of the Complete Science Fiction Stories of Raymund Eich.

www.ingramcontent.com/pod-product-compliance
Lightning Source LLC
Chambersburg PA
CBHW032224190726
48289CB00007BA/2378